White Christmas Watched

Stories of
Christmas Miracles
and Mysteries

Steven Roberts

Outskirts Press, Inc.
Denver, Colorado

While Shepherds Watched
Stories of Christmas Miracles and Mysteries

Front cover photographic image courtesy of Deborah Roberts and Sandra Van Winkle, copyright 2007

Author Photograph Courtesy of Alyson Kennedy and Carpe Librium Booksellers Knoxville, Tennessee

The author may be reached at watson.roberts@comcast.net

Outskirts Press, Inc.
http://www.outskirtspress.com

ISBN: 978-1-4327-1401-7

Outskirts Press and the "OP" logo are trademarks belonging to Outskirts Press, Inc.

PRINTED IN THE UNITED STATES OF AMERICA

Library of Congress Control Number: 2007934871

Other Books by Steven Roberts

Christmas on Deery Street and Other Seasonal Stories.

Best wishes

Steve Roberts

2007

For my children, Nick and Courtney, who are and always will be the light of my life.

Foreword

Miracles happen around us everyday. Some are so subtle we don't notice them, others we just ignore. Mysteries abound. They fascinate us, they challenge us, they intrigue us, and they give us pause. This book is about miracles and mysteries.

Like all of the stories I write there are elements of truth in each of these stories. Like all authors I write about what I know. In most cases the characters are completely fictitious; in some cases they are composites of several real people but do not represent any specific person. If they do it's purely coincidental. The setting for most of the stories is the 1960s, a time of uncertainty, revolution, danger, and awakening for me and my friends.

Each story begins with a passage from the Bible, either from Isaiah or from Luke that captures the essence and theme of that particular story. However, while all are unique in their characters and events, they are tied together by a few central themes that illustrate things we all share. The scripture passages are taken from the New King James Version.

This second collection of Christmas stories would never have been completed without the help and support of others. I wish to acknowledge their contributions here.

Elaine Wilson's editing expertise and literary eye were invaluable in making the rough drafts into polished stories. Alyson Kennedy, Steve Wise, Tami MacDonald, and Austin Gaines, offered important suggestions that helped make the stories better. In addition to their technical suggestions Alyson Kennedy and Tami MacDonald have been constant sources of support and encouragement.

Dr. Allen Wier, a master fiction writer, shared with me his talent and expertise on the craft and art of writing. Whether or not I have been able to take his suggestions and write richer, better stories is another matter.

Bob and Martha Barker, Janice Myers, Judy Ridge, Dr. Bob Parrott, Molly Hyatt, Rick Armbrister, Jim and Nancy Carmen, Sue Piper, Nell Alfaro, Linnie McMillan, Tom Underwood, and Doug and Melissa White have offered support and encouragement in many different ways.

Colleen Goulet, my publishing representative at Outskirts Press, has been much more patient with my constant questions and suggestions than could have been asked of anyone. She is at all times very helpful and a consummate professional.

Rebecca Andreas of Outskirts Press also provided very capable and professional assistance.

John Watson, my best friend for over forty years, has kept me focused and been a buffer against distractions so I could finish these stories on time. He remains my most ardent supporter.

None of this would have happened without the support of my mom, Joy, my sister, Cathy, my brother, Ramsey, and the rest of my family who love and support me without question or condition.

S.E.R.

Gabriel's Trumpet

Gabriel's Trumpet

Oh Thou that tellest good tidings to Zion…
Arise, shine for thy light has come. (Isaiah 11:6)

My mother was a complete sucker for door-to-door salesmen. It didn't matter what they were selling, if we needed it, or if we could afford it, she bought it. Stuff she bought, some things that defy description and purpose, filled every available space in the house. Every closet, the attic, the basement, and under every bed were small appliances, kitchen utensils, countless magazines, beauty aids, and any manner of interesting looking things. Most of them were never used and eventually found their way, unceremoniously, to their final resting place, wherever that was.

My kid brother Timmy and I became the source of ridicule from the neighborhood kids because of our mother's inability to say no to salesmen which later became a great source of embarrassment for me. She desperately wanted us to play the piano but any instrument would do. It was a sign of class and culture and refinement. At least that's what she thought. But learning the piano was out of the question; we simply couldn't afford one, not even an old, used one. Just as she had almost resigned herself to the fact that her sons would be just two more of the unwashed and uncultured masses, Lawrence Gilliland rang the doorbell.

Lawrence Gilliland sold musical instruments and music lessons. He was everyone's idea of a bad door-to-door salesman. If you looked up bad salesman in the dictionary you'd see his picture. He had what my dad called "dunlap's disease"-that is his belly done lapped over his belt. His shirt was always wrinkled and his out-of-style tie reached only to the middle of his stomach. He looked as if he lived in his car and he probably did. The hair just above each ear was combed to the middle of his head and apparently lacquered there. Like two waves crashing into each other, each side curled up and then straight down into a thin mesh of steel wool. I'm sure Lawrence was always one small step ahead of the poor house.

Whether by divine providence, proper alignment of the planets, or just plain dumb luck, this was Lawrence Gilliland's lucky day. By the time he made it to our house he had sold every instrument except two. Since my mother had two sons it was a perfect match. Her dream of her house being filled with beautiful music was about to come true.

Timmy and I were three grades apart in school which meant we walked to school together. It also meant he was my shadow. I tolerated him at home but like all kid brothers he wanted to hang out with the big boys all of the time which of course really cramped my style. No matter what I said or did to him, it always ended the same way-his running to mom crying, "Mom, Georgie's aggravating me."

Our mother was barely five feet tall and petite in every way. There was nothing and I mean nothing about her that was intimidating or threatening. She was very soft spoken except when Timmy insisted he was being mistreated by his big brother.

"Now Georgie, be nice to your brother. It won't hurt you to let him play with you and your friends."

"Aw mom! Why can't he play with his own friends?"

"Because he doesn't have any friends his own age."

"That's because he's so weird nobody likes him."

"Georgie, he can't help being unique."

"Unique? He's not unique. He's weird."

These little exchanges always ended with my mother's coup de gras: "Just wait 'till your father gets home, young man!"

Our father was also small but what he liked to call "wiry." We never really knew exactly what wiry meant; we just knew it probably wasn't in our favor to find out. He had strong arms and hands from years of loading and unloading freight cars for the Southern Railroad. Like our mother, he was neither intimidating nor threatening. But he had a paddle.

This paddle was no ordinary bolo paddle. No, this was a medieval weapon of torture and destruction. It was made from petrified mahogany that was as hard as granite. It was covered with tiny metal barbs that could easily turn your backside into hamburger. Then there was the large spike in the end. We could only imagine what its purpose was. It even had a name-Brutus.

He had never actually used Brutus. He did point it at Timmy and me once which was all we needed. It was like kinetic energy, always ready to use. It was hidden someplace-we never knew and never looked. We had only seen it that one time and even though we saw it we were so scared we quickly averted our eyes. So, the legend of Brutus grew in ferocity each time my father uttered, "I'll get Brutus."

I was the only person to meet Brutus face-to-face. Early one Saturday morning, my partner in crime, Fat Wayne, and I decided to re-enact the assault on Iwo Jima in the living room. We placed our infantry legions in the middle of the floor for a full frontal assault. They were supported by tanks and artillery from the rear. Fat Wayne was the Japs and had to defend Mount Suribachi which was located on the arm of the couch.

When we played army, we played army. No imaginary crap for us, no sir. We had dart guns and slingshots with which to rain our ordinance on our enemy. However, the early hour of the assault required bombs and bullets with less intensity and explosive shock than that which a daytime battle required. This posed a dilemma. We usually shot marbles from our slingshot. Obviously, not a good idea indoors. And errant darts would not bounce off the wall quietly.

"I guess we could just pretend" I said rather disappointedly.

"Are you kidding? We don't pretend! You know that. Was John Wayne pretending when he hit the beach In *Sands of Iwo Jima*?" Fat Wayne retorted in his usual authoritative manner. His ability to distinguish fact from fiction would be my undoing on many occasions.

"Do you see John Wayne anywhere? If we wake up daddy we're dead! And even John Wayne couldn't save us from Brutus." Fat Wayne had never seen Brutus, only heard about it. But the legend was enough to dissuade him.

"I'm hungry" (an hourly response and hence the name Fat Wayne).

"You know where the kitchen is," I said, knowing he was already on his way. Fat Wayne knew where everything was in everyone's kitchen and had free reign in all.

"I've got it," he said wheeling around with a slice of Galaxy Bread spread with mayonnaise in one hand and a knife with a glob of peanut butter in the other. "We can use dough balls. Think about it. They won't come apart when they hit something, they can't break anything even from the slingshots, and they won't make any noise if they hit the wall. And you have a whole loaf." It was an uncharacteristic stroke of genius. Usually with food in his hand Fat Wayne only thought and spoke in mono-syllabic grunts.

Galaxy Bread had absolutely no nutritional value. The consistency of the dough was such that you could spread anything on it and not tear holes. It probably had a half-life of five hundred years. We loved it. Mom got it because it was cheap and the bread man brought it to the back door. So, as Fat Wayne stuffed his fat little cheeks with his mayonnaise and peanut butter sandwich, we sat at the kitchen table making various projectiles out of Galaxy Bread in preparation for the ensuing battle.

Our house was the typical post World War II, three bedrooms, thousand square foot, G. I. loan financed house. In other words the rooms were small, the bedrooms were just beyond the living room, and the walls were thin. There was one door separating the living room from the bedrooms. Armed with several hundred Galaxy Bread bombs each, we went to lay siege to the living room island of Iwo Jima.

We each loaded our slingshots and stretched the rubber bands to the max.

"One, two, three" we said in unison and then let

fly the initial volley and the battle, complete with sound effects, was on.

Anytime Wayne and I were on opposite sides we were very competitive. I should have remembered that. He was a bad loser and an even worse winner. So, he was either whining about losing or rubbing it in about winning. The Japanese were winning, which greatly intensified the decibel level of the machine guns and explosions. The more of my men he killed the worse he got. My frustration level was increasing exponentially. But I knew if I blew up the flag on top of Mount Suribachi he'd at least shut up for a while.

I hurriedly compacted five dough balls into one for maximum effect. I put my atomic bomb in my slingshot, took aim and let go. The instant I fired, the hallway door opened and there stood my father, right behind Mount Suribachi like Zeus looking down from Olympus.

Thud!

Apparently, oxidation changes the molecular structure of Galaxy Bread. Rather than a pliable, doughy, harmless ball, what I shot was a white rock. It didn't hit my dad but it would have been better if it had. Rather, it hit the wall just beside his head (I blame my frustration for my bad marksmanship). It didn't ricochet off the wall but buried in the plaster sending plaster dust and Galaxy Bread chips everywhere, including on my dad.

As the dust settled on the couch and my father's underwear all he could see were dough balls and army men covering the living room floor, and me standing there with slingshot in hand. Fat Wayne had vanished. What happened next lives on in the lore of our neighborhood.

Without a word my father disappeared into the hallway. *Had I been spared? Was he simply too tired to do anything?* I turned to run out the door and join the circus but something grabbed my arm and whirled me around. And as I whirled I caught a glimpse of my dad as he and Brutus started their downswing. Just as Brutus was about to take its first bite out of my butt I flinched.

Thump! Crack! Crash!

Sounds not normally heard in nature came from deep in my throat.

Screams. Sobs. Gasps for air filled the room.

It seems when I flinched I altered the trajectory of impact just enough so that it missed my cheeks. Brutus hit squarely on my boney hip. Apparently, Brutus hit my hip in the weakest spot of the wood with enough force to split it completely in two. The laws of physics then took over and the split half sailed through the plate glass window with a very loud crash.

I was floundering around on the floor like a fish out of water uttering great heaves of pain. Fat Wayne was cowering under the kitchen table speaking in tongues anticipating his punishment for the Battle of Iwo Jima Revisited. My father stood in the middle of the room, his body quivering like Jell-o, alternately looking at me flailing away and at the other half of Brutus in the front yard. In addition to plaster dust and Galaxy Bread chips, he was now covered with slivers of glass that twinkled in kaleidoscopic splendor in the morning sun. He was frozen, completely pale, the remains of the once and mighty Brutus still firmly clinched in his hand.

Enter my mom.

God only knows what it must have sounded like to her. I'm sure she thought her family was being massacred in the living room. As she rushed into the room my father turned, only to be looking down the working end of his twelve gauge shotgun. The one he had instructed her to use in case of a break in.

"You don't have to aim. Just put it to your shoulder, point, and pull the trigger. Shoot first. Ask questions later," were the only instructions she had received. All she saw and heard was her son crumpled on the floor and a figure standing over him who was obviously the source of his agony.

Being the well-trained combat veteran he was my father yelled "hit the deck" just as my mom fired.

Whoom!

Double-ought buckshot whizzed over our heads and sprayed the room, taking out Grandma's antique china on display in the corner cupboard and the photograph of my mother's last family reunion, the only one with all her siblings and both of her parents.

She had never fired any weapon, much less one as big as she. The recoil sent her flying backward

11

against the couch just underneath the Galaxy Bread blast. And there she sat. Shotgun between her legs, her hair and face sprinkled with plaster dust, dazed. Then it became deathly silent, except for Fat Wayne's whimpers from the kitchen, and remained that way for what seemed to be three or four hours.

By now everyone was beginning to regain their composure. My father and I were waiting for my mother to react, but she just sat there doing and saying nothing. The incident had completely destroyed the living room, family heirlooms, and the only complete picture of her family. And of course there was my crushed hip. Then the most unexpected thing happened.

My mother stood up, put the stock of the shotgun under her arm as if she had carried one all of her life, and took a thorough panoramic survey of her house. *What was she going to do: shoot my dad? Shoot me?* I had no idea and I'm not sure she did either.

"You boys are going to have to clean this mess up before you do anything else today," and then she left the room. She never mentioned it again.

"Are you all right?" my father asked as he got to his knees.

"I think so."

"You and Wayne wait for me at the kitchen table. Then we'll clean this place up. I'm sorry I hurt your hip, son" and he left the room to face the music with my mother. It was not until years later that the incident ever came up again and we learned of the debriefing between my mom and dad.

***

I had wanted to play the trumpet ever since Reverend Lonnie Latimore did the Easter revival at Broadway Baptist Church in 1962. He was a sight: white suite, white shirt, white tie, and a red carnation in his lapel. He preached and played and played and preached. I wasn't the least bit interested in his sermon. But when the good reverend put his golden trumpet to his lips it was like Gabriel himself came down from heaven and stood right there in the pulpit. In fact, he billed himself as Gabriel from Galveston.

From that moment I was hooked. I bought every record of Miles Davis, Donald Byrd, Freddie Hubbard, and of course Gabriel from Galveston, I could afford, which was very few. If I was at home I was playing them. It drove everyone crazy, especially Timmy, which was one of the unexpected perks.

It happened on a Thursday, Black Thursday as it became known. It was the day Lawrence Gilliland rang our doorbell. By the time he got to our house the informal neighborhood communications network had prepared my mother to make her dream of having cultured sons come true.

Fat Wayne was waiting on the sidewalk when we got to his house. "A band instrument salesman has been in the neighborhood. Everyone's got a new one."

"Whaddya get?

"A trumpet."

"A trumpet? A trumpet? Whaddya mean you got a trumpet? I want a trumpet. You don't even want to play any instrument."

"Better get home. He's at your house now. Maybe he's got another one."

I set a new land-speed record for the last four blocks home. When I burst through the door there was Lawrence Gilliland on the couch watching our mom sign the contract. I quickly surveyed the living room for anything that looked like it might be a trumpet case. Nothing.

In front of the couch were what looked like two instrument cases. One was a long rectangular case too long to be a trumpet. The other was this huge square looking case, also obviously not a trumpet.

"Boys, this is Mr. Gilliland. He sells musical instruments. And guess what-Santa has come early this year." *Had he ever!*

This can't be happening I thought. *Fat Wayne got my trumpet.*

"Timmy, this is yours," she said pointing to the long one. "Open it up."

It was a trombone.

Momma beamed with delight. "Play it, Timmy."

Of course Timmy had no idea what to do. Mr. Gilliland had to help him place the instrument and position the mouthpiece which completely covered his whole mouth.

"Now blow." And with a big gasp Timmy blew

as hard as he could and managed a faint, metallic squeak. The mouthpiece, however, was not the only obstacle-there was manipulating the slide. If stood on end the trombone was taller than he was. And his arms were too short to move the slide out of first position. Becoming a trombone virtuoso wasn't looking very good.

Timmy could care less about playing any instrument, but he saw this as a chance to butter-up mom. "I love it, Mom. I'll play for you anytime you want. And when I get rich and famous I'll take you with me all over the world." She beamed even more.

"Now you, Georgie. The big one's for you."

Since my instrument was obviously not a trumpet, I wasn't the least bit interested. I had no idea, however, the loathing that would soon exist between me and the contents of the mystery case.

I could hardly pick it up. So, I pushed it to the middle of the floor and positioned the case on its back. Just as I flipped the clasp, both sides flung open revealing my musical future.

There it was, in all its glory and splendor. A Model 2353 Hohnica Keyboard Accordion, complete with thirty-four treble keys, three sets of reeds, and seventy-two bass buttons, the concert grand of accordions.

"Oh, Georgie! Isn't it wonderful. Mr. Gilliland says it's just like having a portable piano you can take everywhere.

IT'S AN ACCORDIAN! Not a portable piano.

An accordion, I wanted to yell but didn't.

"Pick it up. Put it on. Play something." She was standing now clapping her dainty hands together in front of her chest.. "Oh son, I'm so happy."

I couldn't pick it up much less put it on. With Mr. Gilliland's help I managed to get the straps over my arms and stand erect. I thought my chest would cave in any second. He stood behind me and together we pulled and pushed the bellows as I pushed the keys. My mother was simply overcome with joy. You'd have thought Van Clyburn was performing in our living room.

"Oh, Georgie, it's just wonderful" was all she could say.

Mr. Gilliland helped me put the accordion back in its case. And in a matter of minutes he was off to celebrate the best day of his career. More important than selling all his instruments, however, was the fact that he was able to unload the one instrument no one ever wanted-the accordion and I was the proud recipient.

***

Elmer Pollard, the Minister of Music at our church, quickly heard about the events of Black Thursday. Being the ecclesiastical opportunist he was, he announced the next Sunday morning that he was starting the Pollard Conservatory of Music for all children wishing to learn to play an instrument. *How timely and generous,* I thought.

That was all every mother in our neighborhood had to hear. We were all signed up, for a small weekly fee, of course, for lessons with Mr. Pollard every Tuesday after school. Never mind that he studied vocal music and could barely bang-out a few basic chords on the piano. When I pointed this out to my mother her response was, "Well, he went to music college, he has a beautiful voice, and he's a minister of God. The Lord will work it out." Her logic was lost on me.

So, Timmy and I became the first students of the Pollard Conservatory of Music, which was a terrible misnomer, unless a bunch of school kids sitting in the same room blowing and plucking, or in my case squeezing, all at the same time with little or no instruction is a conservatory. But it looked really good on his resume.

Every Tuesday Timmy and I hurried home to get our instruments, load them in our trusty Radio Flyer, and pull our musical future past all of our friends' houses to church. The Fogarty boys became the ridicule of the neighborhood. Every street, every corner had kids waiting to taunt and laugh. These were the older neighborhood kids, the ones we couldn't beat up, who saw their harassment as a matter of personal honor and a generational right of passage. Impervious to weather, these kids never missed a Tuesday for months. Oh, the things we do to please our mothers.

As time passed the novelty of Timmy and me pulling our wagon filled mostly with my accordion

17

wore off and the big kids found other ways to make our live miserable. Our weekly lessons at the Pollard Conservatory of Music were rudimentary at best. Mr. Pollard either knew enough or researched enough to show us proper positioning, basic movement, fingering, and instrument care. He was pretty good teaching us to read music, so all wasn't lost. But we were pretty much on our own. I must have played the C and G major scales a million times.

I left every lesson angry, angry at my mom and especially at Fat Wayne. He never touched his trumpet except at lessons and then only barely. It was a sacrilege the way he disrespected my trumpet. My trumpet. He should have been stuck with this stupid accordion that I had to play sitting down because it was too heavy to stand up for very long. To Fat Wayne it was just a horn. That's it. Since we were best friends he let me hold it and finger the valves. When I did, it was like holding the Holy Grail.

Mr. Pollard knew how much I wanted to play the trumpet and took pity on me. I stayed after Tuesday lessons and he showed me what he could. I soaked up every word, every note, every technique. Of course, this extra instruction cost me dearly. Since Timmy had to wait too, there was his fee to keep quiet and Fat Wayne's rental fee. The two took most of what I made carrying the morning paper. What was left went toward song books and my own mouthpiece. Fat Wayne never cleaned his. There was always this brown substance inside the lip of the mouthpiece. No matter what I used to try and clean it-Clorox, steel wool, hydrochloric acid-it never came clean. Since I knew some of the stuff he put in his mouth, oral hygiene and disease prevention demanded my own mouthpiece.

Under the cloak of new-found religious zeal I took every opportunity to stop by the church and practice the trumpet. And the accordion, too, just to make my mom happy. How she loved to hear Timmy and me play. It didn't matter that we could only play scales; we were playing instruments which meant class and culture to her. Being the trustworthy kid I was, Mr. Pollard gave me a key to the music room so I could practice whenever I had time.

Fat Wayne's trumpet and I established an instant rapport. Mastery came quickly. It wasn't just a horn as it was to him; it was part of me, an extension and expression of my soul.

***

Like most churches the Christmas and Easter cantatas were the highlights of the musical year at Broadway Baptist. Elmer Pollard now had a new means of "packing 'em in" for this year's Christmas program. He had learned early in his career that having kids perform at least doubled the typical attendance. He was sure the sanctuary would be filled to overflowing this year. Who was the guest

19

soloist for this year's program? None other than Gabriel from Galveston himself, Lonnie Latimore.

Our little ensemble consisted of a trumpet (Fat Wayne, not me), a trombone (Timmy), a violin, a snare drum, a tuba, an electric guitar, a piccolo, and the ole Hohnica accordion. We were the only ones who could play the melody to "Silent Night," our contribution to the program which was to occur right before the grand finale. For kids who mostly taught themselves we didn't sound all that bad.

The anticipation of getting to be in the same program with the man who started it all was almost more than I could bear. As soon as I got up each morning I'd mark off the day on my mother's calendar in the kitchen. I thought the performance day would never arrive.

Mr. Pollard got our mothers to provide a reception, punch and cookies mostly, for Mr. Latimore before the program. Refreshments also helped to pack the pews. It meant that I could actually meet him-Gabriel from Galveston.

"Lonnie, this is Georgie Fogarty. He's quite the budding musician" Mr. Pollard said as Gabriel stuck out his hand.

Georgie? Why did he introduce me as Georgie. I'll never be considered a serious musician if everyone keeps calling me Georgie.

"And what instrument do you play, Georgie?"

Before I could say, "Trumpet, just like you," Mr. Pollard beat me to the punch.

"He plays the accordion"

ACCORDIAN! ACCORDION! Oh the shame of it. Introduced as an accordion player to Gabriel himself.

"I see. Never liked the accordion much, myself. Too much oomph-pa-pa for me." Then he turned to chat with Wanda Wilson whose red, low-cut mohair sweater, at least two sizes too small, caught his eye.

I was crushed. My fate was sealed. I'd grow up and live out my days wearing lederhosen playing in a polka band in some Scandinavian restaurant where the waitresses said "Yaw, for sure," in a thick accent.

***

Lonnie had several solos each leading to the big finale-Handel's Trumpet Voluntary and Hallelujah Chorus. But this was not the Lonnie Latimore I was accustomed to hearing. His trills didn't have the crisp triple tongue work he was famous for. Something was wrong. And then it happened. Lonnie quietly left. He was positioned in the baptistery so it was easy for him to sneak out without being seen. I saw it. Mr. Pollard saw it. Just as Mr. Pollard began to realize his ticket to a much larger church with a much larger and more accomplished choir flushed from his future just as the color had flushed from his face, Lonnie was in the men's room flushing the remains of Wanda Wilson's homemade fruit cake surprise.

Mr. Pollard caught my eye and motioned with

his eyebrows for me to find Lonnie. It's impossible to be quiet or discreet when handling an accordion. So, I waited for Eloise Tarwater to begin her aria. She had a big voice with a wide vibrato that whorbled loudly. I knew she'd cover whatever noise I made leaving.

I found Mr. Latimore in the floor of the first stall, his arms around the commode, and his head resting on the seat uttering "Take me now Jesus, take me now." It was clear Gabriel had played his last note of the evening.

I hurried back to the sanctuary to tell Mr. Pollard that there would be no Hallelujah tonight. Then the strangest thing happened, something I didn't understand then and don't really understand now. As I tried to get Mr. Pollard's attention, I noticed Lonnie's trumpet lying on the floor next to his music stand. Without thinking I picked it up, worked the valves up and down a few times, and then stood there motionless. Just as the Conservatory Ensemble finished Silent Night I put the golden instrument to my lips and as if on cue began Handel's Trumpet Voluntary.

I was actually pretty good at sight reading but this was way beyond me. I had never seen the music before or even heard it before but it flowed from my lips and fingers as if I had played it a thousand times. It was like I was in some kind of trance. I don't remember thinking or reading the notes. I just played. Every note, every measure was perfect. If I didn't know better I'd have said the trumpet was playing itself. Of course everyone thought it was Lonnie playing. No one knew it was me; no one except my dad, who had slipped out when he saw me sneak out. He saw my whole performance and I never knew it. When I finished I was exhausted and exhilarated, confused and awe-struck. I had sight read both pieces perfectly.

Just as I finished, Mr. Latimore sort of staggered up next to me. He looked terrible and smelled worse, but he was at least standing and not begging for the second coming. He looked as bewildered as I'm sure I did. Then Mr. Pollard called for him to step out to receive his praise from the audience who immediately gave him a standing ovation. He looked at me, shrugged and said "Sorry kid, better luck next time" and began bowing as if he were meeting the Queen of England. We both knew his little secret was safe; no one would ever believe it was me and not him playing. But I would always know and he would always know and that was enough for me. No one seemed to notice that I had been absent from the ensemble, not even mom.

Dad helped me load my monster instrument into the trunk of the car, something he had never helped me with before. All my mother could talk about was how wonderful Lonnie Latimore was.

"Wasn't it just thrilling! What a talent! God really smiled on us tonight."

If you knew about Wanda Wilson and her Fruit Cake Surprise you'd be singing a different tune, I thought to myself.

"Georgie, if you could only learn to play your accordion like that."

Now *I* needed to throw up.

"That's enough, Erma," my dad said from no where.

***

Although I was excited when Christmas Day arrived it was anti-climactic. I had received my gift at the concert. For those few moments I was as good as Miles Davis and Freddie Hubbard and all the other great trumpeters of our time. Even as great as the Reverend Lonnie Latimore.

The Christmas morning ritual at our house was that my dad played Santa and gave everyone a present. We each took turns opening ours so that everyone could see who got what. As my dad gave me my last present he placed it beside me and then put his hand on my shoulder and gave me a little squeeze. This was completely out of character for him. He was not an affectionate man, certainly not with me and Timmy.

When it was my turn I cautiously unwrapped the gift and revealed an instrument case. I quickly flipped open the clasp. There in my lap right before my eyes was Lonnie Latimore's Amoti B flat, Tomoni Kato design trumpet. Mom and I looked perplexed at the trumpet and then at Dad, who just sort of grinned at me. And then I knew that he knew. Not knowing what to say no one said anything.

Later as they were in the kitchen preparing dinner, I overheard them talking.

"Why'd you get him a trumpet when he has an accordion?"

"Erma, the boy wants to play the trumpet."

"How do you know?"

"I just know. Besides, I traded the accordion for the trumpet."

"You did what?"

"That's right. I traded the accordion for the trumpet. He hates the accordion. He only plays it to make you happy. Besides, he can't even stand up with the dumb thing." Then silence fell over the kitchen.

I just sat clutching the trumpet, my trumpet, periodically working the valves up and down. Not until many years later did I learn that my dad had made an agreement with Lonnie after the performance; his silence and the accordion in exchange for the trumpet. Apparently, the phrase "front page scandal" caught Lonnie's attention and sealed the deal.

That evening as we all sat in the living room in the glow of the tree my father said something he had never said before: "Play something, Georgie," as he handed me the trumpet. From that Christmas on until his death, every Christmas night he would say "Play something Georgie." Then as everyone settled in for the night I and my trumpet, that used to be Lonnie Latimore's, brought the celebration and solemnity of the day to a close with a heart-felt and very grateful Hallelujah.

Peace in the Valley

Peace in the Valley

Now there were shepherds living out in the fields,
Keeping watch over their flocks by night. (Luke 2:8)

Sunrise over the An Lo Valley in the Central Highlands of Vietnam is fantasy. No smell of gunpowder or the fumes of napalm. No whop, whop, whop of the daily helicopter blades that disturbed the sounds of jungle creatures going about their 100 million-year old survival routine. Foe and friend alike are still in the half-sleep of war, the one eye open-one eye closed, semiconscious state that offers no rest and only momentary relief. It is hard to believe that the Eden-like valley at sunrise will soon be filled with the concussion from high explosives, the rat-a-tat-tat of gunfire, and the cries of the wounded and dying. However, each day begins the same way-the horrors of the previous day

29

erased and a new slate, a new chance offered by the first rays as they illuminate the momentary peace in the valley.

***

First Platoon, Charlie Company, Fourth Infantry Division and parts of the Fifth Regiment of the North Vietnamese Army had chased each other in a deadly game of hide and seek up and down the Valley for the past two months. Casualties were significant on both sides. First Platoon was always the lead element, always assigned the most difficult missions, and was always asked to pick up the slack for the other platoons. It had the lowest casualty rate of any platoon in the entire regiment, not because they didn't see action (they saw more than anyone) but, quite simply, because of 1st Lt. Frank Johnson and Staff Sergeant Lyle Underwood.

Frank Johnson was a likable kid whose round baby face belied his extraordinary instincts and courage in the heat of battle. He had spent his whole tour of duty "in the bush" turning down opportunities to have less dangerous positions in a much safer environment. "If I'm going to be a soldier, I'm going to be a soldier," he was fond of saying. He was, quite simply, a born leader.

Lyle Underwood was a career soldier in every sense of the word. He didn't tell jokes with the men or discuss their personal lives. He was all business-the business of keeping them alive. Highly decorated, he was first and foremost a combat soldier. Because of the paper work and mickey mouse procedures associated with desk jobs, which for him was anything not in the field., he hated being stateside. He'd get bored, get drunk, get in fights, and end up in the stockade, which is why he was still a staff sergeant and had three ex-wives. But put him in the field, especially in combat, with a platoon of men and there was no one better. This was his third tour in Vietnam.

Lt. Johnson and Sergeant Underwood became acquainted on Johnson's first assignment at Ft. Polk, Louisiana, a horrid place where the mosquitoes were as big as crows and could suck your veins dry in a matter of seconds. It was the last stop before being sent to Vietnam. When they saluted and shook hands for the first time there was an almost audible click; the one every officer and every sergeant wish for and few get; the one that binds and bonds in unexplainable and unfathomable ways and creates true comrades, true brothers-in-arms. Thus began the unique relationship between them.

Being under their command was a blessing and a curse-they were the best leaders and because they were their platoon saw more action. They rarely got to stay in base camp for more than a night or two. Then God smiled on them in the form of a new company commander, one who knew something about leading troops in combat. First Platoon was rotating back to Fire Base ALV (short for An Lo

Valley), the home of the 16th Artillery and the sometimes home of Charlie Company. And they would be there for Christmas.

The fire base was located on top of Hill 531 and commanded a clear view of the valley and the Ho Chi Minh Trail. Not too long ago the whole valley had been thick jungle like much of the highlands. Most of the vegetation especially along the tops of the hills had been obliterated by artillery fire and B-52 strikes. However, the undergrowth-bamboo, scrub trees, elephant grass-had re-grown along the banks of the An Lo River and almost half way up the hill creating an odd sight-plush green and desolate brown.

Right below ALV was a Montagnard Village. Montagnards were indigenous tribes that still hunted with bows and arrows, and moved with amazing stealth throughout the Central Highlands. They didn't particularly like Americans, but they hated the North Vietnamese (NVA) and the Viet Cong (VC). The proximity of the village to ALV was a double-edged sword. The Americans looked after them-sort of protection by default-but American assistance also created greater threats from the NVA and VC who were notorious for their methods of slow, agonizing torture for those who helped the Americans, especially the tribal elders and their families.

***

There's a strange dichotomy all combat soldiers

experience between their killer life, the one every soldier has to create for himself in order to do the unspeakable things soldiers have to do, and their human life, the one they left and hope to return to but never can because that life has been forever changed. There was no better example of these warring selves than the two-headed monster known as mail. Everyone loved getting it and some even passed their letters around. But reminders of life back home were also reminders of life in the jungle. The emotional gyrations of instantaneously jumping between the Killer Being and the Human Being simply required too much energy and made each soldier emotionally vulnerable.

Frank's wife, Abby, was really good to write every week and send a package at least once a month, sometimes with chocolate chip and peanut butter cookies (which were mostly crumbs by the time he got them), sometimes hard candy and gum, and always letters and the Sunday funnies. He'd eat a few of the goodies and save a few for later. The rest he gave to Sgt. Underwood to share with the troops, with instructions to keep their origin anonymous. But they always knew.

About one week before Christmas, Frank received his Christmas package from Abby. Mailed in October, it had made the rounds through the army's esoteric mail system and, surprisingly, had arrived with the contents in tact. There was a Polaroid picture of Abby wearing a provocative red silk gown and a Santa hat with the inscription, "I've been nice-waiting to be naughty," across the bottom. It contained twenty-four Christmas drawings, one from each of her first graders on the same type of ruled learning-to-write paper all students have used since paper was invented. Each had a depiction of Santa, or the manger scene, or the wise men riding camels with three or five legs following a huge star. But there was one that instantly captured his imagination and heart.

It was a picture of shepherds watching over their sheep on a hillside. Two small angels hovered above the flock pointing toward a bright, shining star bathing Bethlehem in light in the distance below. The shepherds, angels, and sheep appeared to be three dimensional. The star and Bethlehem portrayed accurate size and distance. Written across the top in better-than-average lettering was "Peace In The Valley" by Joshua. It was by no means a typical first grader drawing.

In addition to the usual contents was a neatly wrapped box which contained all the parts necessary to construct a Christmas tree. There were several cardboard tubes from rolls of toilet paper and paper towels; rolls of aluminum foil, a container of glitter, several dispensers of tape, pieces of coat hangers to construct the base and the tree limbs, red and green pipe cleaners to cover the limbs with; and a star. And of course there were detailed instructions of how to put it all together. It had been Joshua who had suggested they make the tree for Frank.

Frank found the time to put the tree trunk together and attached it to the base. He had Sgt. Lockwood put the tree and all the decorating supplies in the communications bunker which was located in his platoon's area. He instructed Lockwood to tell the men to finish decorating the tree. As always, the cookies were distributed among them.

As they had a chance the men would go to the commo bunker, take a piece of coat hanger, wrap it with the red and green pipe cleaners, and insert it into the trunk. A creative assortment of ornaments hung from the red and green tree limbs: pictures from back home, a small copy of the Twenty Third Psalm, a couple of C-ration can openers, a pair of paratrooper wings, a green and white Fourth Division patch, various rank insignia, and dog tags of fallen comrades. They had also decorated the bunker with the Christmas drawings. The men loved it. Yes, it reminded them of where they were and where they weren't. But there was something peaceful and therapeutic about the atmosphere it all created, something intangible but very real. Something that gave them pause and peace if only for a few minutes.

For this year's Christmas the Division Commander ordered that the troops of the Fourth Division were to observe a quasi-cease fire. What this meant was no offensive action Christmas Eve and Christmas day-no patrols, no ambushes, no action that required being in the jungle; everyone was to be at their base camp or fire base for these two days. While not standard operating procedure it was not unheard of. And any reason not to have to go out was always welcomed by the men.

***

Corporal Juan Alvarez Martinez (JAM for short), First Platoon's Radio-Telephone Operator (RTO), was from a wealth family in San Juan, Puerto Rico. He spoke three languages fluently; unfortunately, English wasn't one of them. They were Spanish, Mandarin Chinese, and Vietnamese. His father owned an international import-export business. As a result his family spent more time in Southeast Asia than in Puerto Rico. When he first entered the Army, he was a scout/interpreter. By the time he reached Vietnam and First Platoon he was a RTO. How he came to be a radio operator in the United States Army and not speak English is a well-kept secret. When asked he'd shrug and say "Don't know."

Because of his linguistic aptitude and skills he caught on to conversational English quickly. It was Army English, with its funny acronyms and special terms he never got. As an RTO he was worthless; he couldn't even carry the platoon radio. He was forever getting the antenna caught in the thick undergrowth of the An Lo Valley, requiring assistance from someone else or taking the radio off to get untangled. However, as an interpreter he was invaluable.

Juan could hang around prisoners and listen to their conversations without causing alarm. Since he obviously wasn't Vietnamese they spoke freely around him. He acquired critical information without lifting a finger. There's no telling how many lives Juan saved, and there's no doubt he was a big part of First Platoon's success.

Mortar fire was commonplace at all base camps and firebases. Those accustomed to being on the receiving end could tell, with a fairly high degree of accuracy, where the rounds were going to land simply by the pitch of the whistle they made. Mortar rounds move more slowly through the air than artillery rounds. It was not all that hard to actually see them: look toward the sound, then quickly move your eyes ahead of the sound and you could find them.

Depending on the base camp's size, location, and permanency, latrines varied in their construction, appointments, degree of privacy, and number of soldiers accommodated. Since First Platoon wasn't at ALV much, its latrine was basically an outhouse without the house. It was surrounded by ponchos stretched between tent stakes. It provided for two people to sit back-to-back. There was no roof.

Not long after lunch on Christmas Eve JAM made his way to the latrine, a roll of toilet paper in one hand, *Popular Mechanics* in Spanish, in the other. Without the regular afternoon shelling it was actually fairly quiet.

Thump! The distinctive sound of a mortar round Being launched from its tube disturbed the setting.

Everyone immediately looked toward the escarpment of the closest hill across the river, waiting for another thump. Then came the whistle as the round moved through the air.

JAM, engrossed in his magazine, missed the thump but heard the whistle. Like everyone else he looked toward the sound and then moved his eyes ahead. And there it was: a small, dark object traveling through the arch of its trajectory on its way back to earth.

JAM went back to his article and then suddenly looked straight up. It was coming right at him. Paralyzed by fear, he sat there mumbling consecutively in all three languages. The closer it got the louder he mumbled. By this time everyone in First Platoon's area was following the mortar round on its way to deliver its Christmas message to Juan Alvarez Martinez.

Thud! All took cover.

Nothing. Everyone waited a few seconds and then raised their heads.

"AHHHHHHHHHHHH!" JAM ran through the poncho walls, *Popular Mechanics* in one hand and his pants, that he had managed to pull up between his knees and ankles, in the other, now screaming in all three languages at once, with a little English mixed in to boot. Past the chopper revetment, past number one gun placement, down the main trail, through the barbed wire he ran still clutching his pants in one hand and the *Popular Mechanics* in the other until he disappeared down the side of Fire Base ALV headed toward the Montagnard village.

Everyone stood motionless and speechless, mesmerized by the sight of Juan running (running was not what he was doing but there really isn't a word that accurately describes his movement). Then, without exception, everyone burst into laughter. Johnson and Underwood quickly sought to take control.

"Sergeant Underwood, we still have a round in the latrine," Frank said, trying to summon some kind of serious tone.

By this time Underwood had fallen to his knees trying to keep from falling over completely in belly laughter. All of First Platoon was overcome with side-splitting laughter. They beat their palms on sand bags, leaned on ammo crates to keep from falling down, held their sides in pain, and slapped each other on the backs . It was all Frank could do not to join them.

"Lyle," Frank said realizing there was still a mortar round in the latrine. "We've gotta get rid of that round. It may still be live."

"Yes, sir. I understand sir. I'll take care of it, Lt." he gasped in between laughter sobs.

"And send someone out to look for JAM."

"But Lt., the old man said no patrols. And when he says no patrols, he means no patrols." Frank's suggestion to disobey the no patrol order snapped Underwood out of his laughing fit.

"We can't leave him out there. Give me three guys and I'll go. Watson, Irwin, and Hunter are good."

"Lt., you can't be doing that. I'll go."

"Staff Sergeant Underwood," he said firmly. "You take care of the round in what's left of the latrine. If anyone's gonna get canned for disobeying the old man, it'll be me."

"Yes, sir."

There was a brief silence and then Underwood spoke.

"Can you imagine? Sitting there taking care of business. And looking up and watching this mortar round come straight for you and you knowing you're about to die in a really awful way. And you keep following it until it lands between your feet. You sit there waiting for it to go off and it never does. Can you imagine what must have gone through his mind?"

Then they could stand it no longer and burst out laughing, spewing snot and spit as they relived watching Juan Alvarez Martinez tear through the fire base, *Popular Mechanics* in one hand and his pants in the other, headed for some unknown destination.

"Musta been a hellava article," Underwood quipped as they both started preparing to conclude the "Incident at ALV Latrine."

Lt. Johnson and his unauthorized patrol found where JAM entered the jungle. Usually they followed blood trails. Not this time. No, this time they followed another kind of human trail. Once in the jungle all signs of Juan disappeared. Frank was torn. He didn't want to leave Juan God-knows-where, but he also didn't want to end up in Long Bin Jail. And they were ill-equipped to engage the enemy if that become necessary. They searched for about an hour and then returned to ALV.

Back at base, things had calmed down. Sgt. Underwood had disposed of the mortar round. Turns out it was a dud. Some of the men of First Platoon were manning typical security locations while the rest were in their bunkers hoping for an uneventful Christmas Eve and Christmas Day.

Regardless of where they finished for the day, Frank always made the rounds among his men. He'd go to each of the security positions.

"You guys got everything you need? Water? Ammo? Playmate-of-the-Month?"

"Sorry, Lt. She musta been in the latrine with JAM," the M-60 machine gunner responded.

They all snickered. Frank couldn't help but worry about Juan. He could be a royal pain in the neck but he was one of his guys, and he really liked him.

"Keep your eyes wide open tonight. If the NVA finds out about the ceasefire we could be in big trouble."

Both Lt. Johnson and Sgt. Underwood thought the ceasefire was a terrible idea. While it resonated with some of the men, it also left ALV vulnerable, more so than usual. They both had an eerie feeling.

As Frank continued from position to position he stopped to observe the sun setting over the mountains of the An Lo Valley. It was a beautiful sight, one he rarely got see. It could have been any one of a thousand valleys in his beloved East Tennessee mountains.

"Lt! Lt!"

Frank turned toward the supplication from Oliver Smeltzer, the company clerk who was filling in as the radio operator.

Before he could speak Smeltzer began, "Lt., he's back!"

"Who's back?"

"JAM! He's back. He just showed up. Sgt. Underwood's got him in the commo bunker."

"He's back? Where'd he come from? Is he alright?"

"He came from the Vil. Looks pretty bad and smells worse."

By the time he made it to the commo bunker Sgt. Underwood was in the process of cleaning Juan up. A nasty looking and smelling pile of jungle fatigues was in the corner. One of the medics was giving him the once-over. Johnson pulled Underwood aside.

"What's the doc say?"

"He's fine. Still rattled from the mortar round. Guess I can't blame him. Keeps mumbling alternately in Spanish and Vietnamese something like 'they're coming. They're coming. Too many. Gonna destroy the vil' or something like that. Lt., I think there's something to it."

Frank walked over to him, grabbed an empty ammo crate, and sat down on it face-to-face with Juan. He leaned over, forearms on his knees. Took Juan by the arms as if he was his own son.

"Juan, I want you to listen to me." His voice was soothing but obviously serious. "Tell me exactly what you're mumbling about. Is it something you saw? Something you heard?"

"They know about the cease fire. They're coming for us and the vil at the same time. The vil is a decoy. When we move to defend the vil they'll hit us from the north slope. There's at least a regiment on the other side of the river." It seems that when Juan finally collapsed from his spontaneous scenic tour of the An Lo Valley it was just below one of the exits from a tunnel complex that ran throughout the valley. He could hear the sounds of rifles being loaded, and the small talk some soldiers use to overcome the anxiety of imminent battle. Most importantly, he could hear the battle plans being discussed.

"When are they coming?"

"Now. They're coming now." The words hung in the air like an imaginary neon sign flashing in electric colors "They're coming now." Fortunately, "now" really didn't mean immediately but soon. And where they were coming was right at First Platoon.

"We're dead," Underwood said, rather matter-of-factly.

"No we're not! I'll think of something. Go get the Captain."

"Not here."

"Where is he?"

"All officers captain and above are back at Division for a surprise Christmas dinner. They left while you were out looking for Juan. Hadn't had a chance to tell you."

"Well, who's in charge?"

"You are."

"WHAT!"

"Yep. You're the ranking officer. You get to be in charge of what's lining up to be a blood bath and we're the ones getting washed."

"Don't these idiot people comprehend that we're in a war and we're standing up here on this stupid hill all by ourselves with the bad guys breathing down our necks. And they're back at division kissing the old man's butt?"

"That's about the size of it."

"Try to get the captain on the horn. Get me the other platoon leaders and the chief of the gun crew. Meet me back here in 30 minutes. And get Juan dressed and back here, too. He's staying with me."

He sat back down on the ammo crate. He knew that if he didn't come up with a master plan quickly the villagers would be massacred and ALV would be overrun. If that happened the NVA would control of the whole valley. Frank took a deep breath and looked at the Christmas tree sparkling in the last rays of the day. His eyes took a brief survey of all the first grade drawings and then stopped on his favorite, the one from Joshua.

"That's It! That's It!"

***

"Everything ready?"

"We've got everyone we could find out of the village. They're stuffed in every bunker and hole possible. There may still be a few left."

"Can't help that now. Whatever happens to them will be a damn sight better than what the NVA would do to them."

"Lt, I sure wish you'd come back up the hill. This is suicide."

"You and I are the only ones who can pull this off. If I'm to coordinate this fiasco it has to be from here. And I need you up there."

"Frank," Underwood paused. He never called him by his first name.

"Sgt. Underwood."

"Yes, sir" and he climbed back up the hill.

The plan was simple in design-bold and very risky, but simple. It was the execution that was tricky. Second Platoon would evacuate the village as quickly and quietly as possible spreading gasoline everywhere as they left. They also left C4 charges in strategic locations. They would blow the village just as the NVA arrived. Second Platoon's commander was against it, said it was too risky. Their disagreement lasted long enough for Frank to say, "I'm not leaving the villagers to be butchered. You will evacuate the village! You will do it quickly and quietly. And you will do it now or I'll turn you over to the NVA myself!"

All of the mortar crews would plot coordinates along the north slope and the village. Four 105mm howitzers would plot coordinates on both side of the river. The coordinates were such that they could walk rounds all the way up the hill if necessary. The remaining two howitzers would be positioned along the perimeter pointing down the north slope and would fire at point-blank range. It was a bold, very risky plan indeed.

Frank had positioned himself half way down the hill and half way between the village and the north slope. He could see everything from there. He would also be caught between both forces for the duration of the battle. It was he and Juan and the radio. ALV was out numbered three-or-four-to-one. He hoped the element of surprise would compensate. Three M60 machine gun crews with all the ammo they could carry were positioned in fifty yard increments down the north slope. Frank would give the order for the first crew to fire. When the NVA got close the crew would retreat back to the perimeter and then the second would fire. Then the third crew would pick up after the second crew finished. It was the men of First Platoon who were outside the wire and who were manning the perimeter of the north slope. They had all volunteered. Everyone knew that those outside

ALV had the odds really stacked against them.

"Juan, I hope you're right, because if you're not, we'll all be dead."

"Trust me, Lt."

Frank got Underwood on the radio. "You ready?"

"We're ready. Quick Lt, check out the vil."

Through his starlight scope he could see the NVA approaching the village. He switched his view and saw the lead element beginning to cross the river and head up the North slope. Frank knew that they wouldn't attack the village until most of the main force was on the North slope. He wasn't going to let that happen. The key was knowing when to pull the trigger.

Next, he got the first M60 crew on the radio. "You ready?"

"Ready, Lt."

"When we light 'em up hit 'em with all you got. Spray everywhere."

"Roger."

"Lt! Lt!" Juan was shaking all over.

Frank could see that the diversion group was inside the village. He pressed the transmitter on the radio.

"Now."

Thump-Thump-Thump-came the sounds of illumination rounds firing out of the mortar tubes. And then the sky was almost like day. The M60 opened up. White phosphorus rounds exploded in their characteristic star-burst on both sides of the river. Then came the high explosive rounds.

Thump. Thump. Thump. More illumination rounds exploded overhead.

Frank kept switching from the village to the north slope. The NVA were getting close to the first M60.

"Get out now," he commanded through the radio microphone. In a matter of seconds the first crew was up the hill and the second crew had begun firing.

Frank couldn't help but notice that the red tracer rounds from the 50 caliber machine guns firing into the village and the green tracer rounds for the M60s looked like strands of Christmas tree lights stretching down the hill from ALV.

His plan was working perfectly. The second crew had finished and the third had begun. The village was completely in flames. Those in the diversion force were either dead or were retreating back across the river. Because of the artillery fire only a small portion of the main force had managed to get across the river and only a few had made up the hill at all. However, they were able to advance some in the lull when one machine gun crew stopped firing and the other began. He knew that some would make it close to the perimeter when the third crew withdrew. He also knew he and Juan would have to hold their position regardless of what else happened. He was the eyes, Juan was the ears.

Sure enough, when the third crew withdrew, the number of NVA soldiers running up the hill increased dramatically.

As planned the illumination rounds had stopped. The tubes of the howitzers were pointing straight down the hill. For an instant everything stopped and became completely silent.

"Lt., they're getting ready to charge up the hill," Juan whispered in his broken English.

Frank keyed the microphone.

"Now," he whispered.

Thump. Thump. Thump.

It was daylight again. The NVA began charging up the hill screaming as loudly as they could.

Frank rolled on top of Juan. "What are you doing?" Juan whispered.

"Saving your life. Now shut up."

Just then the howitzers fired. Thousands of tiny razor-blade-like projectiles filled the air, making distinctive thuds as they ripped apart anyone on the north slope. The mortars were walking their rounds up the hill while the other four howitzers pounded both sides of the river.

It was hard to know when to give the cease fire. After a few minutes of constant firing from the perimeter howitzers Frank raised up enough to look through the starlight scope but it was hard to tell who was dead and who wasn't. Those who could walk were trying to retreat back across the river only to be caught between the mortars and the howitzers. He could hear Sgt. Underwood calling on the radio but one of the razor blades had split the microphone cable in two. He knew Underwood wouldn't let up as long as the bad guys weren't back in the tunnels.

After a few more minutes the firing stopped. He waited for it to begin again. Then he realized it was over, at least for the time being.

"Come on, Juan. Start crawling back up the hill."

"Okay, Lt."

As he attempted to move Frank felts sharp pains in his left thigh and left ankle. He looked down. His pant leg was covered in blood. He could see parts of the razor blades sticking out of his leg in several places.

"Juan, you go on. I'll catch up."

"No sir, I know what you're doing. I'll drag you if I have to but you ain't staying here. And if you give me any trouble I'll shoot you myself." Together they slowly began making their way back up to ALV. They hadn't gotten very far when they heard people coming. They froze.

"You boys having fun rolling around in the dirt?"

They both let out a huge sigh. It was Underwood. They were now surrounded by men from First Platoon

"Help the lieutenant. I'll take Juan. He and I have developed a close, personal relationship today. What is it with you, always running around in the jungle?" Underwood quipped.

Juan just grinned.

***

Although they required over one hundred stitches, Frank's wounds were not life threatening. He refused to leave ALV for medical attention, saying, "the aide station is good enough." He was the only casualty of the battle. A few mortar rounds managed to hit but caused little damage. Just as the medic finished sewing him up Sgt. Underwood walked into the aide station.

"Lt., don't you think you need to medivac out to the hospital. Those are some nasty wounds." He was right. Frank had several deep cuts in his thigh, one that almost went from hip to knee. He also had a puncture wound just above his ankle and a few cuts along his shin.

"I'll be fine. What's the damage?"

"None of our guys got hit. None of the villagers either. Not a scratch on anyone. Aside from screwing up the barrels of two howitzers and burning up some M60s, you and the commo bunker are the only casualties."

"Not the commo bunker."

"Yep. Took a direct hit. Didn't do much, though. Here, I'll help you. You need to see something."

Underwood helped Frank up and together they walked the few feet to the commo bunker. As they got closer he heard a strange sound. It sounded like a baby.

There in the commo bunker was a young couple: a girl who looked to be seventeen or so but was probably younger, and a young man maybe in his early twenties. She was holding a baby wrapped in a sheet from the aide station. Beside them was the Christmas tree and above was the picture of the shepherds.

"She went into labor right after we got all of the villagers inside," Underwood said. "Doc delivered the kid. Happened during the first barrage of illumination rounds. One went off right over head. It would've been nice to have had JAM up here to interpret instead of goofing around in the grass with you."

Just then the young mother held up the baby and offered it to Frank. He was surprised by her gesture. He took the baby in his arms and began rocking it back and forth. Then he realized it was Christmas morning.

"You know Lt, you saved this couple and their baby. You saved the whole village. Without you they'd all be dead or wish they were. But you saved them. Us too. We'd have been overrun for sure. Just like in that picture over there. You were the…"

"Shepherd?"

"Yeah, shepherd."

Frank bent down and gave the baby back to its mother who bowed her head respectfully. She said something in Vietnamese. He looked at Juan. "She said 'Bless you, sir.'" He bowed toward the mother and child.

Just then the first rays of the sun burst into the bunker casting a golden glow around the mother and baby. The father stood up, removed the leather bracelet (a symbol all boys get when they become men, sort of a Montagnard Bar Mitzvah) from around his wrist and hung it on the tree.

Frank began to take it all in. He went over and took down the picture of the shepherds and limped out of the bunker, taking another look at the baby's face as he did. Underwood followed.

"I didn't ask, is it a boy or girl?"

"It's a boy," Underwood said. "We named him Joshua."

Frank put his hand on Underwood's shoulder and gave him a little squeeze. Then he walked to the edge of the perimeter and looked out over the valley as he held up Joshua's picture. Underwood knew not to follow.

Like every morning it was silent except for the jungle creatures. The sounds of the wounded and dying were gone. No chopper blades, no explosions, no gun fire. The smell of gunpowder was whisked away by the morning breeze. The valley was new-born. For that moment and for the next few moments, there would be peace on earth.

Miracle in the Clearing

Miracle in the Clearing

The wolf shall lie down with the lamb...And a little child shall lead them. (Isaiah 11:6)

Arnie Alred was a tragic figure. Tall, stocky, and strong, he was imposing. He was twenty years old, could grow a full beard in a day and a half, and spoke very little. When he did he mostly mumbled to himself. We never knew what world he was in, we just knew he wasn't in ours.

He had a strange look and an even stranger demeanor. He had this psychopath, ax murderer grin all of the time especially when he walked taking his big giant clumsy steps. He couldn't carry on even the most basic conversation but it didn't matter because everyone was so afraid no one wanted to talk to him. While he looked like a man he was actually a small boy. We met Arnie in Mr.

Davenport's seventh grade Geography class.

There we were listening to Mr. Davenport talk about how Russia's horrible winters helped defeat Napoleon and Hitler when Miss Brixie, the principle, called Mr. Davenport outside. After a brief discussion Mr. Davenport came back in leading Arnie by the arm.

"Class, this is Arnold Alred (his name didn't register until it was too late). He'll be joining our class for a while. Please make him welcome."

Arnie slowly surveyed the room with that look of his. His eyes were vacant one minute, piercing the next. We all slumped in our desks hoping he'd miss us. We didn't know who he was and we didn't care. He obviously wasn't a student. *Maybe he's a student teacher. Yeah, that's it. He's a student teacher* I thought. Then as if through instantaneous telepathy we all looked at each other and thought the same thing: *we're doomed.*

Arnie took his seat at the end of the first row just inside the door. We were all equally terrified and, at the same time, fascinated by him. He was just so strange, unlike anyone we had ever met. We'd all quickly glance his way then just as quickly look back at Mr. Davenport. I was drawn to him from the start. I don't know why.

My glances kept getting longer. I wondered why he looked like that, like he's alive and dead at the same time. Then his eyes caught me and I thought I was going to throw up on my hand colored map of Eastern Europe in 1942.

Rumors quickly spread through the school about the mean, grizzly new kid who'd been in prison since he was twelve. And not reform school either. According to the rumors he'd been in solitary confinement at Brushy Mountain Maximum Security Prison for the last five years. He was in school as part of an experiment to see if the most hardened murderers could actually be put back into society and function in a civilized manner. And he was in our first class every morning. *Well, he's sure not a student teacher.*

"Did you hear about the murderer in school?" queried Billy Wakefield, the leader of our gang?

"I didn't have to hear. He sat three rows over from me in Davenport's class."

"I heard he whacked each of his parents forty times with a hatchet," Billy continued.

"That was Lizzie Borden, you dummy."

"What difference does it make? I heard he killed them both and then smeared their blood all over his face and then drank it."

"You're crazy."

"Well that's what I heard." Thus the legend of Arnie Alred grew to epic proportions in just a few hours. I had no idea the impact Arnie would have on my life.

One morning before class I was spinning my lucky Eisenhower silver dollar on top of my desk. I caught Arnie out of the corner of my eye. He was coming toward me. I just knew he'd grab me by the hair, drag me into the boy's bathroom, slice me into little pieces, and flush my remains into the sewer.

"Hi Arnie," I squeaked. He just stood there looking at the silver dollar making a circle with his finger. I put the dollar on its edge, held it at the top with one finger, and then flicked it with another. His eyes followed every turn with complete fascination. When the coin stopped he'd motion for me to do it again. This went on several more times. I knew it was about time for the bell to ring. When the last spin stopped he reached for the coin.

"No, you can't have it." *I'm dead! He won't even drag me to the bathroom. He'll slice me up right here.* I looked up at him. He looked dejected. I removed my hand from over the dollar. He picked it up, smiled down at me, and went back to his desk. He began spinning the coin as I had done. The first few times it fell on the floor but he managed to do it after about four tries. *A small price to pay for my life* I thought. *Stupid good luck charm didn't work anyway.*

***

To be cool and tough you had to be in a gang. Our gang was more like a loose-knit association. We liked to think we were tough but we really weren't. We did have a gang-like name though-the Knights.

Like all self-respecting, bonafide gangs we had membership requirements, officers, initiation procedures, a membership oath, and a hang-out house. It actually wasn't a house. It was Billy Wakefield's father's utility shed. Mr. Wakefield apparently knew something of the sociological importance of adolescent boys forming peer groups.

Mr. Wakefield turned the shed over to us with the understanding that we would clean it out, find uses for the tools inside, and keep the place clean. He even installed a couple of extra electrical outlets so we could have more light than just the one bulb hanging from the middle of the ceiling.

It was not a large building but it was large enough to accommodate about a dozen boys. We were able to acquire from family discards a couple of couches, a few chairs, some lamps, and a desk to keep our important stuff in. The gang leader, who we called the Head Knight, was Billy Wakefield solely because of the shed. Billy got to sit behind the desk and act important which he took every opportunity to do. We had regular meetings and talked about things to do which wasn't much. We just wanted to feel grown up.

Our meetings were mostly a chance for us to get together and talk about the things near and dear to our hearts-girls and sex. Of course we knew absolutely nothing about either. We did, however, have our sources.

Joe Spooner's brother was in the navy and provided Joe, and thus the rest of us, with all manner of photographs and illustrative diagrams. Doyle McIntyre's brother was eighteen and had gone steady with several girls known in the boys' bathroom for their willingness to assist in male sexual education. By the time we got this kind of information it had gone through several tellings and adaptations and most likely had no basis in fact. Unfortunately, guys like Doyle's brother ruined the reputations of many girls just so they could look studly to their friends. However, our most regular and dependable sources of information were Roger Fini's father's collection of "girly" magazines, and Buddy Alexander's sister's book entitled *You're Becoming a Woman*. Between the two we had some basic and general idea of the female body and the purpose of its unique parts.

As much as we loved to talk about girls and sex there was one subject that superseded all others and required immediate attention-our rival gang, the dreaded Tacoma Street Boys. Like all feuds we had no idea why we hated them and they hated us. We just did. The Tacoma Street Boys were tougher, stronger, and meaner but we were smarter and more clever-a classic clash of brawn versus brains.

Our two neighborhoods were separated by a buffer zone of undeveloped wooded land that ran from the back of our neighborhood to the front of theirs. We called the area the "Weeds." It was about four hundred yards deep and about one hundred yards wide but seemed much bigger. There was an imaginary line that established our respective domains-the top half was ours, the bottom half was theirs. We didn't venture into their side without dire consequences. They didn't come into our side much, although they could have whenever they wanted to. When they did it was usually to use us in preparation for engagements with real gangs.

The Weeds had several huge Red and Pin Oak trees scattered about but it was by no means a thick forest. It was mostly filled with underbrush, Mimosa trees, and various weeds that grew to be much taller than us. We had developed an intricate system of paths and escape routes throughout our sector that required navigational skills and local knowledge to avoid getting hopelessly lost in our little jungle. Legend has it years ago Mike Kainer's little brother followed him into the Weeds and wasn't seen again for years. When he finally wondered out his family had moved to Canada. We had look out posts in the oak trees, built fortresses held together by Mimosa bark, and secret passages into and out of the forbidden land of the Tacoma Street Boys.

Alfred Alred was their leader. His mother called him Alfie but he preferred Butch. To be a real gang you had to have a guy named Butch. We didn't, which is one of the many reasons we were never taken seriously in the hierarchy of local gangs. The closest we could get to Butch was Buddy and Buddy just didn't have the same street fighter, death row inmate ring to it that Butch had. Butch became their leader-for-life by employing the most basic Machiavellian principle-eliminate the competition by whatever means necessary. We were about to learn that the Boys had just acquired an enforcer, their own Goliath, in the person of Arnie Alred, the rampaging murderer loose in our school. Arnie was Butch's older brother.

Besides Arnie and Butch there were three older Alred boys. Except for Butch they were no more than fifteen months apart in age. When they were kids they used to put Arnie in the garbage can, put the lid on it, and then beat the sides with baseball bats. Back then garbage cans were fifty-five gallon metal barrels. Apparently, at least according to Butch, the bong, bong, bong that ricocheted and echoed inside the barrel was too much for Arnie, and, as he put it, "made him into a real weirdo." But when the older brothers tried to do the same thing to Butch, Arnie, who at that time was bigger and stronger than they were, broke one's nose, broke one's arm, and knocked the third's front teeth out. From that moment Butch was Arnie's guardian and Arnie was Butch's protector.

Butch took his guardianship seriously. There was no doubt he loved Arnie and had his best interest at heart but he was not above using Arnie's strength and mental deficiencies, not to mention Arnie's complete devotion to him, to his advantage.

***

Christmas, 1963 ended the feud between the Knights and the Tacoma Street Boys. In fact, it was the end of the Knights as well.

Our meager little lives revolved around the Knights. Everything we did had the gang's activities at heart. If we got an extra yard to mow or birthday money it was used, at least in part, to further the interest and reputation of the Knights.

With school out we spent most of our time in the hang-out. Two days before Christmas Buddy Alexander's kid brother, Wally, began banging on the door.

"Open up! Open up! O--pen--up!"

As we opened the door he fell into the hang-out talking a mile-a-minute gasping for breath.

"They've (gasp) invaded (gasp)!"

Billy Wakefield, the Head Knight, took charge. "Who's invaded?"

"They (gasp) have (gasp)!"

"WALLY! WHO'S INVADED?"

"The Tacoma Street Boys!" By this time Wally had caught his breath enough to stop gasping but he was still talking so fast we could barely understand him. But the words *Tacoma Street Boys* made us all pay very close attention. Fear and confusion filled us all.

"Okay, Wally, just calm down and tell us what's going on," Billy declared.

After a few deep breaths Wally made it abundantly clear.

"They've violated the Christmas ceasefire and torn up the fort.!"

"How do you know?"

"I saw them, that's how!"

"Are they still there?"

"I think they went back to their side."

We all began asking, "Are you sure? Are you sure?" in rapid-fire succession.

"Okay! Okay! Everybody settle down," Billy asserted. "What matters is what are we going to do about it?" It was not a rhetorical question.

"I told you! Didn't I tell you we need protection? I bet their parent's are commies," Albert Steiner interrupted.

"Steiner, you're crazy," I interjected. "They may be mean and they may be nasty but they aren't communists."

"How do you know?"

Steiner was born paranoid. By the third grade he bought into Cold War propaganda that communists had infiltrated government offices, police forces, hospitals, the post office, and local churches. He even believed that fluoridation of the public water supply was a commie plot to make us into mindless zombies. He was certain communist spies had killed President Kennedy just a few weeks earlier. He saw a commie behind every tree. He later became president of the local chapter of the John Birch Society.

He was always saying we needed to protect the hang-out and our stuff, and given our lack of physical prowess we needed a gun to do that. We all thought he was nuts and gave no credence to his warnings of an imminent communist take over. He had asked for a "Tommy Gun" for the past few

Christmases but never got one, of course. Since his parents were staunch pacifists the closest he came to getting a weapon was a water pistol. We became very uncomfortable, however, when he showed up one day with a Remington .22 caliber rifle, a hand-me-down from his grandfather and the source of great consternation from his parents. He also had plenty of ammunition.

The Tacoma Street Boys violated the two most fundamental, albeit unwritten, laws of inter-gang relations: no raids on undefended territory and under no circumstances were ceasefires to be broken.

This blatant disregard for honor between gangs demanded a severe and immediate retaliation that sent a clear message: regardless of our lack of muscle the Knights were not to be trifled with. If the truth were known we had done similar things many times, we just hadn't destroyed their stuff and we hadn't been caught in their area. So, we set about planning Operation Christmas Massacre.

We all gathered at the hang-out about noon on Christmas Eve to exact our revenge and strike a blow for kids like us everywhere. As everyone recited his assignment Steiner sat with his rifle across his lap methodically moving the bolt back and forth. Showing clear insight to the severity of the situation Billy told Steiner he was to guard the hang-out thus eliminating the risk of anyone getting shot. Convinced we all knew our parts, and Steiner and his .22 had been neutralized, off we went to defend the Knights' honor and demonstrate that brains and ingenuity can defeat brute strength. At least, that's what we hoped.

Operation Christmas Massacre was simple. Billy Wakefield, through our maze of secret passages, would defiantly go to Butch's house and challenge the Boys to meet us in the clearing where both gangs would do battle face-to-face like real men. Billy delivering the challenge on Butch's front porch clearly indicated how serious we were. They would be unable to refuse even if it was Christmas Eve.

The clearing was an open area where we had chopped down Mimosa trees for the bark to use in various construction projects. It also had an abundance of staubs. Staubs were tall, rigid weeds that could easily be pulled out of the ground. If done properly a clump of mud always remained on the end which made them great weapons: they could be thrown with accuracy, they delivered a pretty good wallop, and the mud exploded on impact momentarily blinding the victim.

Knights were positioned all around the clearing armed with mud balls and giant clods, an array of different sized staubs, spears made from Mimosa limbs, and a healthy supply of firecrackers and roman candles. If the battle went badly, we had cherry bombs. It had rained the day before so the mud balls were easy to compact. We had taken crap from the Tacoma Street Boys long enough. This was it, our line drawn in the sand (or the clearing), our ultimate mice or men test.

The clearing sloped slightly from our side down to theirs. Because I had the best arm I was positioned behind a mound at the top of the clearing which gave me a clear field of fire. It also had the main escape ditch behind it. We had all of their escape routes covered from both sides.

We waited anxiously. My heart pounded in my throat. I couldn't swallow. I could barely breathe. Billy was hidden at the bottom of the clearing along side of the route we knew they would take. We had two or three man teams positioned at equal increments around the clearing. Each team leader would fire the roman candles and firecrackers as the others let fly whatever ordinance they had. Billy would light a pack of firecrackers when the Boys were all in the clearing both to surprise them and signal to the rest of us to rain mud and fireballs down on our unsuspecting enemies surrounded in the clearing.

Max Goode, the smallest and stealthiest Knight, was the communications runner. He also had an accurate arm. He was to make his way through the undergrowth to pass the word "they're coming." When he reached the mound he was to be on my team. With the Boys dazed and confused by the roman candles and firecrackers we would pick them off one-by-one with our earthen bombs and spears. I had a cardboard periscope I bought at W. T. Grants Department Store for fifty cents. I always knew it would come in handy some day. That day was now.

When I saw them enter the clearing I froze. Arnie, the ex-convict from my geography class, was leading the way with Butch safely behind him. *We have to call it off. Arnie would kill us all* I thought. But it was too late. The massacre had been irreversibly set in motion.

I could tell they thought this would be like all the other battles-they'd beat us up and we'd turn and run back to the club house bleeding and bruised and secure in the knowledge that we were no match for the Tacoma Street Boys. And never would be. *We're all dead! We're all dead!* I kept repeating to myself.

All of the other Boys had formed lines on either side of Arnie and Butch and stood in the middle of the clearing oozing with self confidence in what would surely be yet another in a long line of butt-whippings they had inflected on us.

"Come on out you bunch of babies. Let's…"

Rat-a-tat-a-tat-a-tat-a-tat-a-tat.

In a split second Max and I were on top of the mound, arms cocked and ready. Red and green fireballs swooshed from their cardboard tubes and bounced off of the Boys now stunned and bewildered. Staubs rained from the air like arrows from Alexander's archers striking the Boys all over. Mud balls whizzed through the air like cannon balls. The Boys were hoping and jumping and screaming grabbing their heads and arms and stomachs not knowing what to do or where to run. Every exit was caught in crisscrossing mud and fire.

They could do nothing except move haphazardously in decreasing concentric circles.

Max and I were waiting for clear shots. Butch and Arnie were our first objectives. When the smoke cleared enough I took aim. Just as I let loose the staub with the biggest mud clod on the end Butch turned and faced me.

Thud!! It hit Butch right in the middle of his chest. The only sound he made was a whoosh as the air rushed from his lungs as he fell like a rock at Arnie's feet. The force of its impact, and the wet mud, caused the staub to stick to his sweatshirt. There he lay, spread-eagle with the appearance that the staub had gone straight through him.

Arnie bent over to see about Butch. I could see Butch's eyes were open but he wasn't moving. Arnie rose and turned toward me and Max.

Thud! Thud! Thud! Three mud balls in a row. Max's hit him in the neck just below his Adam 's apple. My first one hit him on the left ear. The second one did it-right between the eyes. I could see its impact clearly. But I was surprised to see blood trickling down his nose. Little did I know that Max had put rocks inside the mud balls. The story of David and Goliath rushed through my head as Arnie slumped to his knees. When they saw their leader and champion both on the ground the remaining Boys ran through the weeds and briars clearing new paths on the way to safety back on Tacoma Street.

We jumped and yelled and shook empty roman candle tubes at them and held staubs high above our heads in victorious salute to our cunning and courage. We would become legends in gang lore. Kids would move out of our way in the hall as we passed by. The Christmas Massacre would be told for generations. Our manhood was established.

Just as the rush from our combat victory reached a fevered pitch Arnie rose to one knee and then stood up. He looked down at Butch who was now trying to suck in what air he could, still lying with the staub sticking straight up. *Goliath isn't supposed to get up* I thought to myself.

Everything got quiet. Blue-ish white smoke swirled above the clearing as it weaved through the few over-hanging tree limbs. Then Arnie began walking slowly toward Max and me. His look was one I had never seen before, one that made me want to wet my pants. I was frozen. Max collapsed and rolled down into the escape ditch. *I'm about to die* was all I thought.

Butch had managed to catch his breath enough to get to his knees and utter as loudly as he could "Kill 'em, Arnie."

Crack! I felt something fly past my ear. Butch screamed and fell to the ground seeking cover.

Arnie was still coming toward me. I heard a sound I had heard very recently.

"I'll show you, you commie scum."

Crack.

Arnie went down this time. I whirled to my right.

"Steiner!" I yelled as I rushed toward him.

Crack.

***

I opened my eyes only to find a stranger's face directly above me. Arnie was looking over his shoulder. *I'm in hell. I've died and gone straight to hell. No waiting for the rapture, no purgatory. Nope, straight to hell* I thought. My surroundings were unfamiliar. We were moving but I had no idea how or where.

"How ya doin?" the stranger asked.

"My head hurts and I have this awful pain in my shoulder."

"That's because you've been shot. Clean wound, though. Went straight through. You'll be fine."

"I've been what?"

"What's your name?"

"Danny Cochran."

"Danny, can you tell us what happened?

Of course I can't tell you. I didn't even know I'd been shot.

"No sir. I have no idea."

"You think maybe this gorilla behind me did it?"

"I don't know who did but I do know it wasn't him."

"We thought maybe it was an accident. It's the strangest thing though. He shows up at Fire Station 11 with you in his arms. Blood all over both of you. He's been shot, too. Looks like a bullet grazed his head and another went through his shirt pocket. But we can't touch him. We've tried. Thought he'd break my wrist. All he'd say was 'you fix him, you fix him.' As soon as we started on you he let go."

"What about Butch and the others?"

"Who's Butch? There're not others. Just you and King Kong, here."

"You fix him," Arnie said with some authority just as I passed out.

When I opened my eyes again I was greeted by a beautiful young woman with a white pointy hat and starched white uniform. She was putting a bandage over the hole in my shoulder. Her touch was soft and soothing.

"Welcome back, Danny." Her voice was as smooth as a summer breeze.

I'm in heaven. God felt sorry for me and grabbed me out of hell and took me to heaven with this wonderful angel to look after me I thought as I smiled back at her.

"Where am I?"

"The emergency room. Who's your friend here. I need to check him out, too but no one can get close enough to take a look at him. He's a scary guy, you know."

Boy, do I ever.

Just then Arnie's face appeared over her shoulder. "You fix him," was all he'd say.

I wasn't sure what to do. Arnie's face had a look I hadn't seen before. It was fear. He was afraid, but of what? No one was going to touch him; he'd made that very clear.

"Danny, we need to call your parents. We have no information on you. And all your friend will say is 'you fix him.'"

I gave the nurse my number and my parents' names. It took some coaxing from me to get Arnie to let the nurse leave the room to call my folks. Apparently, as long as he thought they were tending to me he was fine. However, if he thought they weren't then he became adamant and demonstrated his super human strength and tolerance for pain

"Your folks are on the way. I didn't go into much detail. I said you were in an accident and a friend had brought you here. I assured them you would be alright. Now, what can you tell me about him?" I know she assumed he was an adult.

"Ma'am, you need to call his mother, too. His name is Arnie Alred. He lives on Tacoma Street. I don't know the address or his mother's name. His house is about mid-way down the block."

"See if you can get him to let me look at his head and chest while I go try to reach his mother. He's got to be in really bad pain."

The nurse left the room. I raised my left arm and motioned for Arnie to come closer.

"Arnie, shake my hand." He took my hand and squeezed it but his touch was as gentle as the nurse's. "Arnie, thank you for saving my life. I'll never forget it. Now, I want you to listen to me," I said as if I were talking to a six year old. "When the nurse comes back I want you to let her to fix your head."

"Fix you."

"They've fixed me. I just have to rest for awhile. I'll be fine. But they need to fix you now." He looked puzzled. "Now that we're friends we have to take care of each other. And since Butch isn't here I have to take care of you. Will you do that for me?"

His expression instantly changed from concern to almost joy. It was hard to describe. Then he said, "Okay, they fix me."

He remained at my side holding my hand until the nurse returned.

"There's no Alred on Tacoma Street. We have no idea where to go from here."

"That's okay, I'll take care of him. He says you can fix him now. Arnie, this very nice nurse is going to look at the cut on your head. She won't hurt you (*I wish I hadn't said that-it's gotta hurt*) and then you need to take your jacket off. Okay?"

He nodded slightly and said "fix me now."

The nurse came over to him and attempted to take his hand out of mine. She gave him that same disarming smile as she gave me and he released my hand.

"Will you take off you jacket for me, Arnie?" her voice as soothing as ever. I nodded in agreement and he took it off. "Now Arnie, I need for you to take your shirt off." Even I could see where the bullet had gone through his shirt pocket. Again, he did as was requested. He seemed embarrassed to be naked from the waist up in front of a woman.

"That's funny. There's no wound. Not even a scratch, not a red mark, nothing. Hum?" Then the nurse moved her attention to the cut on his head. "This will be fine. It doesn't even require stitches." She cleaned his head and closed it with several butterfly strips. After he put his shirt back on he came over to the bed and took my hand again and simply said "friends."

It wasn't long before my parents showed up. My mother was absolutely beside herself. Of course we hadn't said anything about the Christmas Massacre, and since Arnie had taken me to the fire hall no one knew where I was.

"Oh my baby, my poor baby," she said trying to hug me.

"Ow! That hurts momma."

"Who's this?" she said looking at Arnie.

"He's a friend. He's the one that got me here. It's a long story."

I over heard the nurse telling my dad that I needed to stay overnight. They wanted to give me strong antibiotics and watch me to be sure my wound didn't get infected. I'd be moved to a regular floor in a little while.

"Dad, could you come over here, please?" My father had yet to see my protector. He was taken aback at Arnie's size and apparent age.

"This is Arnie Alred. He lives on Tacoma. I don't know which house (Billy Wakefield was the only member of the Knights who knew where he lived). You need to take him and try and find his mother. Call the Wakefields if you have to. His mom doesn't know where he is either."

"Okay, son. C'mon Arnie. Let's go find your mother." But Arnie wasn't leaving. My dad tried to tug on his arm a little which brought a take-your-hand-off-me-before-I-break-your-arm look. Arnie grasped the rails of the bed so hard I thought he'd break them in two. "Just leave him here and go find his mother," I said.

It wasn't long before an orderly came to take me to my room.

"Whatever you do let Arnie, here, go with us," I told the orderly. "Let him hold onto the rail and we'll all be fine." With that we were on our way to my own hospital room complete with my mother and Arnie Alred.

Not long after I got to my room my dad came in. He had no luck finding Arnie's mother. It wouldn't have mattered. Arnie wasn't going anywhere that I wasn't going. "The Wakefields weren't home either," my dad said. I was sure his family was searching for him and had no idea where he was or that he was safe with me. My dad didn't stay. Someone needed to watch my brothers and sisters, and help Santa. So, my mom stayed.

It wasn't long before my mom fell asleep in the chair. Arnie stood beside my bed standing guard. The events of Christmas Eve were still fuzzy. I had figured out that Steiner shot me instead of Arnie. *But what about Butch and the rest of them?* I also figured out why he took me to the Fire Hall. It was the only place he knew where people would help me. *He walked over two miles carrying me* I thought in amazement.

I could see the Christmas lights from down town through my window. "Look Arnie, don't the Christmas lights look nice?" He turned to look out the window. When he turned back he took off his jacket and unbuttoned the top shirt. When he got to the second shirt he reached in the pocket and took something out and then put it in my hand. It was my lucky silver dollar with a .22 slug buried in Dwight Eisenhower's head. "That's why there was no wound" I said out loud. All Arnie said was "Merry Christmas."

***

Not long after we got home Butch knocked on our door. He saw Arnie and ran up and hugged him. I explained what had happened, that Arnie was alright, and that we had tried to find them. Even when Butch tried to take him home he wouldn't go until I said it was alright.

Everyone blamed Arnie for what happened. No matter how hard I tried to explain he wasn't the culprit, no one believed me. And none of us told the truth about the massacre either-it was a matter of honor, the unwritten law.

When they left my house that Christmas morning it was the last time I saw Arnie. The little experiment of putting him in a regular classroom for a certain period of time each day had failed badly. I didn't understand until years later why Arnie was put into our class at all.

He was institutionalized in a state hospital where, as I understand it, he spent the rest of his days. Although I think of him often, each Christmas I get out the silver dollar that probably saved his life and spin it on the table. While it's spinning I say a little prayer: "Thank you for fixing me, Arnie. Thank you for showing true friendship. Thank you for teaching me the transforming power and grace of unconditional love and the real meaning of Christmas. I love you, Arnie, wherever you are."

The Madam and the

Paperboy

The Madam and the Paperboy

For unto us a child is born…(Isaiah 9:6)

£ very town, at least in the South, has a house that everyone knows about but no one talks about. Our town's was Miss Maybelle Boudreaux's house, a large, three-story colonial at the dead end of Third Avenue. Silent Alley, as it was known, ran behind the house connecting Second and Fourth Avenues. It wasn't like most alleys; it had one purpose-silent and concealed access to Miss Maybelle's. At one time it was just a path but over the years it became much wider as more and more of her special friends, as she called them, came to visit. Eventually, one of these special friends, the road superintendent, had the alley paved and promised to keep it in good shape in exchange for her loyal friendship and her silence.

The house was on a cul-de-sac and gave the appearance of royalty. In some ways that was true. The grounds were immaculately kept with gardens and beds everywhere. In the spring when the dogwoods, azaleas, and tulips were in bloom is was breath-taking.

Miss Maybelle was a large woman with more chins than you could count. Big fat flaps hung from the underside of her arms and swayed back and forth when she moved. She was always impeccably dressed in the latest fashions though not expensive or fancy. She wore very tasteful jewelry and just the right amount of make-up. She never wore heels. Given her size she still moved with grace and poise, albeit slowly.

She knew all of the rumors, all the stories, all the dirt on everyone in town. What she said was gospel. Though not boastful, she readily admitted she knew the truth about every scandal, every shady deal, every cheating husband, and every alcoholic wife in town. She knew where every skeleton was buried and who buried them. She had special friends in every high position in business and government. I delivered the morning paper to her house.

For the longest time I thought it was a women's boarding house and I suppose it was. I also thought that since laundry was always hanging on the lines out back, mostly sheets, Miss Maybelle's girls took in laundry. I suppose that was true, too.

I, as were all of my friends, was under strict instructions never to go near her house, except to deliver the paper. The penalty for doing so was unspeakable pain and torture. I was never told why. But my friend Johnny Walker had the straight scoop from his father.

Johnny overheard his mom and dad talking one night. He heard his father say, "It's simply awful what happened to Reverend and Mrs. Barnett. Simply awful. How could a man of God, one who quotes scripture with such passion, give in to the temptations of the flesh like that? And poor Mrs. Barnett. I'm sure she's just sick to death. This will kill her. I bet they'll be gone soon. Something's gotta be done about that house and the pain it causes."

That's what went into Johnny's little brain to be analyzed by his less than average intelligence. What came out of his mouth to me was "I heard my dad tell my mom that Reverend and Mrs. Barnett are dying. They both have some horrible disease that he got ministering at Miss Maybelle's and then he gave it to his wife."

"What?"

"Something like polio or TB or some other community disease that's real easy to catch. It's so bad that he got it from knocking on the door."

"You're crazy! You can't get sick from knocking on somebody's door."

"Well, my dad said he took his preacher's duty

of laying his hands on sinners far too literally, whatever that means. And that it was his uncleanness that made his wife sick."

Now, I didn't know much but I did know that you can't get sick from knocking on someone's door.

"You better be careful when you collect for the paper" was Johnny's admonition to me.

I never had to go up to the house. Behind the house was a mailbox at the edge of Silent Alley and her parking area. It was used solely to leave messages to her special friends and vice versa. The mailbox had a flag on each side. If there was a message for her the blue one was up; if there was a message from her the red flag was up. The nature of these messages was known only to the recipient. A smaller, rectangular box was under the mailbox for the newspaper. She'd put my money in an envelope marked "paperboy" and put it in the same place. So, I never met her, saw any of the girls, or had to worry that Johnny Walker's father might be right. I felt pretty safe.

My paper route gave me a sense of independence and responsibility. Each week my mother made me put 10% of what I made in savings and 10% in the offering plate at church. My grandfather would laugh and smirk when I'd figure out what my earnings were. "Better get used to payroll deductions, boy. It gets worse," he'd say every week.

***

I grew up in a house full of women. My mom and I lived with my grandparents and a variety of her sisters; the number varied depending on who was unemployed or unmarried at the time. My grandparents, Ester and Estes Edwards (I called them Ma and Echie), had five daughters-Buena, Gladys, Annalee, Jocelyn (my mom-Echie called her Betty but no one knew why), and Catherine. They were no more than two years apart in age. All beautiful women, they were a hodge-podge in looks. Buena, the oldest, was a tall, slim redhead. I never met her but I had seen her picture, one my mother kept in her dresser drawer. Gladys and Annalee were short, dumpy blondes; and my mom and Catherine were short, slim brunettes. Everyone said Buena was Echie's favorite because she was just like him-tough, stubborn, and uncompromising.

We lived in a typical working class neighborhood just beyond downtown. Gentrification had been attempted several times with only minimal success. Most of our neighbors were what Echie called "time card punching, lunchbox totting, working stiffs" who worked hard everyday of their lives, except for two week vacations at Myrtle Beach each summer. They raised their children in the same manner. All of the houses were small, one level with the same basic floor plan.

There was always a running battle between my aunts. Someone was always mad at someone else. Their arguments were loud and punctuated with a lot of door slamming. They yelled at everyone except my grandfather. No one raised their voice to him much less argued with him. Fortunately for my aunts and mom he worked everyday and wasn't there much. They never agreed on anything, especially on how to raise me. On that subject they each held very strong opinions.

I never knew my father. He died when I was a baby. No one talked about it much, especially my mom. From what I could gather he and my mom caused a family scandal. Regardless of who I asked about him they'd all say "Ask your mother," who'd respond with "I'll tell you when you're older." However, whatever my mother did couldn't compare to the scandal Aunt Buena caused.

One spring Sunday afternoon Aunt Catherine, my favorite, was sitting on the front porch reading the newspaper. Everyone else was either gone or taking the traditional Sunday nap.

Here's my opportunity I thought.

"Aunt Catherine, will you tell me about what happened to Aunt Buena?"

She dropped the paper below her eyes, puzzled by my question and how to respond.

"Some things need to stay buried."

"No body tells me anything! No body has told me anything about my father! No body has told me about Aunt Buena! All I get is 'wait 'till you're older'. Well, I'm older and still no body tells me anything!" I said with as much righteous indignation as I could muster.

"You're right. You're absolutely right. You should know about your own family. I'll make a deal with you. I'll tell you about Buena and I'll tell your mom to tell you about your dad. Fair enough?"

"Fair enough."

"Go into my room and get me a pack of cigarettes. Then make sure Papa is still asleep. And fix me a glass of tea, two sugars, one lemon."

Off I went on little cat feet and returned in record breaking time with Pall Malls and ice tea firmly in hand.

"He's still asleep."

"If Papa wakes up then the story is over, no questions asked."

"But…"

"No questions."

She lit a Pall Mall, took a big swig of tea, then a big drag on the cigarette.

"Buena ran away from home when she was eighteen because Papa wouldn't let her date a boy named Slick, who was exactly what you'd expect from a boy named Slick.

"One Saturday night he tried to defy Papa's orders by showing up at the front door. None of us, not even Buena, ever went on a date unless the boy came to the door and came inside. As she ran to the door Papa intercepted her, grabbed her arm, and asked where she was going."

"'To meet some friends,' she told him defiantly. I was actually proud of her for standing up to the old goat. The rest of us never could."

89

"'One of them that Slick fellow?' He knew it was. Buena couldn't answer."

"By this time we were all in the living room. Papa released her arm and opened the front door. Buena tried to stop him but couldn't. I noticed he had his other hand in his pocket. He opened the door and was face-to-face with Slick."

"'Buena here?' Slick said oozing with self-confidence."

"'Yes, she's here and she's going to remain here,' Papa said with no inflection or emotion in his voice. 'She's forbidden to have anything to do with you. Now Slick, I'm asking you to leave.'"

"'I ain't leaving without Buena. Come on Buena, let's go,' Slick yelled into the room."

"No one had notice Papa had slipped his hand out of his pocket. Just as Slick tried to push him aside Papa placed his .45 caliber pistol squarely in the middle of Slick's forehead and cocked it. Buena began screaming "'Daddy stop! Oh please Daddy! Don't hurt him! I love him!'"

"Your mother and I were trying to restrain Buena. Annalee, Gladys, and Ma had taken refuge behind the couch, their chins propped on the back.

"I couldn't see Papa's face but I could see Slick's. His eyes were like saucers and he was white as a ghost. He was desperately trying to be tough but failing badly."

"'Slick, the way I see it is this. Now you're trespassing. I'm simply protecting my family from an uninvited intruder. Get this straight, one of two things is going to happen: you're going to leave right now and never have any contact with my daughter again, or your brains are going to be all over the porch,' Papa said as emotionless as ever."

"'You wouldn't dare!' Slick's quivering voice belied his fear."

"POW! Everything seemed to stand still as the shot rang out. The sound of the spent cartridge bouncing of the porch floor ricocheted throughout the room, getting louder with each bounce. Buena gasped and fell to the floor. Your mom and I clutched each other and clinched our eyes tightly. None of us looked at Papa and Slick for fear of what we'd see."

"'Does that answer your question?' Papa said just as matter-of-factly."

"I opened one eye and saw Slick shaking in the doorway, a growing wet streak running down the inside of one pant leg. The .45 was again on Slick's forehead. Then I saw the smoke coming up from the hole in the porch between Slick's feet which were now in a puddle. Then in a snap, Slick was gone.

"Papa turned, gently un-cocked the pistol, unloaded it, and put it back in his pocket. He looked directly at each of us pausing as he passed without saying a word. We all got the message. Your mom and I managed to bring Buena around and assured her she wouldn't be cleaning Slick's brains off the porch.

"As he walked back to the kitchen, no doubt for some of his special medicine that no one could ever find, he stopped and looked down at Buena. In the same tone he used with Slick he said 'Don't see him again, ever. If you do, don't come back,' and walked back to the kitchen just as if nothing had happened."

"Later that night, after everyone recovered, we banded together, for the only time in our lives I think, to help Buena escape. We each contributed some essential item to aid in her soon-to-be life on the lamb with Slick. I gave her money I had been saving. We took a solemn oath we would never, even if tortured, divulge what we did.

"In the morning Buena was gone. Ma was overcome with fear and grief. She cried for days on end. We were proud we had helped Buena defy Papa who didn't know she was gone until supper."

"'Where's Buena?' he asked completely emotionless as the night before."

"No one answered. Ma buried her face in her napkin and sobbed."

"'I asked a question,' his voice a few decibels higher."

"Silence. Before he could speak again your mom spoke up."

"'She's run away, Papa. Left in the middle of the night. Here's her note. Says she loves Slick and is going off with him.' What she didn't tell him was Buena's note also said she'd never come home as long as he was alive. Papa hadn't looked up or missed a bite as your mom was talking."

"She laid Buena's note in front of him. He

paused, stood up, picked up the note without looking at it, walked over to the fireplace, pulled out his lighter and lit the note, and placed it in the fireplace. Then he walked back to the table, picked up Buena's chair, walked to the backdoor, and threw the chair into the alley. We could hear the wood crack and shatter as the chair hit the ground. Just like nothing had happened he returned to the table, sat down, and looked at each of us just as he had the night before."

"'Buena's dead.' Then he finished his supper."

"Everyone knew we were forbidden to mention her name or anything about her. I don't remember ever hearing Buena's name in his presence again. Of course we'd talk about her and try to guess what kind of life she was having. We just knew her life was filled with romance and adventure, and total adoration from Slick.

"She'd send Ma a postcard fairly often, ones you can find in most any drug store. She knew Papa wouldn't be home when the mail came. Ma hid them in the inside pockets of her winter coat. After a few years the cards stopped. And when they did Buena was gone forever.

***

I never had to worry about Miss Maybelle not paying. My envelope was in its place every week without fail, except for the week after Halloween. I figured she was out of town and forgot to take care of it before she left. While I needed the money I wasn't about to ask for it. Then when it wasn't there the next week I became worried. I couldn't let her go two weeks without paying-it was simply bad business. So, the next Saturday morning I summoned every ounce of courage I could possibly summon and rode my bike to Miss Maybelle's to collect for the newspaper.

As I peddled I kept thinking *what if Johnny Walker's father was right? What if they did have some dreaded, mysterious disease? What if I could catch it from the door knob? What if someone sees me? Should I stop and get some gloves and a surgical mask?* I was tormented by uncertainty and fear.

As I approached the steps that went to the second floor where the backdoor was I noticed two beautiful, young women hanging laundry on the porch. They both had on white, cotton gowns and were barefoot. I could partially see the silhouette of their young, sleek bodies as the morning sun shone from behind them. I tried not to look. *What am I doing? Being two weeks late isn't worth dying for* I thought as I climbed the stairs. When I got to the back porch they were waiting for me.

"You're awful cute," one said as they both walked toward me.

"Thank you, ma'am," was all I could say. My heart was beating so fast I was surprised I could speak at all.

"And sweet and polite, too," the other said as

the both reached to take each of my hands.

That was it. Down I went. Out cold.

When I woke up one of the girls was holding a cold cloth on my head while the other was holding my hand. As I looked up all I could see was a mammoth woman who seemed to reach all the way to the ceiling standing over me.

"Who are you, young man? " Miss Maybelle asked.

"Sonny, Sonny Suffrage. I'm the paperboy."

"Girls, help Sonny Suffrage up and sit him on the swing then go inside. One of you bring our new friend a glass of lemonade."

Without hesitation they did as they were told but not before kissing me on the cheeks simultaneously. After just a few sips of the lemonade my head began to clear. Miss Maybelle stood in front of me in her best matronly pose and expression.

"How are you feeling?"

"Much better, thank you ma'am." Realizing where I was, my heart started racing again. "I better get going. I have other houses to collect from."

"Collect from? Is that why you're here, to collect for the newspaper?" She was not happy.

"Yes, ma'am. It's for two weeks."

"Two weeks!"

"Wait here, Sonny Suffrage. I'll be right back!"

She disappeared through the back door. In just a few seconds I heard a very loud "Adele, get down here!" Then in another few seconds I heard feet hurriedly coming down a staircase. And in another few seconds Miss Maybelle burst through the backdoor pulling a young woman by the arm.

"Adele, this young man is Mr. Sonny Suffrage. He has his own business the same as you and I. *I'm Mr. Suffrage the business man now. I like how that sounds.* He's here to collect for delivering the newspaper. I owe him for two weeks. Could you explain why young Mr. Suffrage hasn't been paid?"

"I simply forgot, Miss Maybelle," Adele said as she tried to cower at Miss Maybelle's feet.

"Would you allow one of your clients to forget to pay you?" Miss Maybelle answered for her. "Of course not."

"Do you still have the money?"

"No ma'am."

"Go inside and get your purse so you can pay Mr. Suffrage." Her tone was serious not angry.

Adele quickly went into the house and almost as quickly returned with her purse.

"Give me the two weeks payment I gave to you to leave in the box. Then give Mr. Suffrage triple what we owe him." *Triple? They're giving me triple?*

Without question, without hesitation she gave Miss Maybelle her money and then turned and handed me my money.

"Now, do you have something to say to Mr. Suffrage?"

"Mr. Suffrage, I apologize for being two weeks late paying for the newspaper. I promise it will never happen again. Will you accept my apology?"

"Yes ma'am."

"Thank you, Adele," Miss Maybelle said politely. Adele was back inside bounding up the stairs before the door could slam.

'Sonny, I'm sorry about this." *Back to Sonny again.* "I've been out of town. I told Adele to be sure you got paid."

"It's okay, ma'am. And I'm sorry I got so nervous and passed out."

"Why were you so nervous?"

"I've never been to a house like this, you know, where people talk about what..." I began stammering here.

"What goes on here?"

"Yes, ma'am."

"Tell you what. You come back tomorrow after Sunday dinner and I'll tell you what really goes on here."

She reached out her hand. "By the way, I'm Maybelle Boudreaux." As we shook hands I noticed a sparkle in her eyes that wasn't there before. She patted my hand as we walked to the steps, like my first grade teacher did when she walked us down the hall.

"Thank you for everything, ma'am."

"Until tomorrow afternoon, then?" It was more of an invitation than a declaration.

"Yes ma'am, I'll be here." I had no idea how I would get there but I wasn't about to tell her no. One word from her about my little fainting episode and my reputation was ruined. I mean, there I was on the back porch of Miss Maybelle's, two beautiful young women eager to assist me, and I passed out. I would never over come the shame and humiliation. No, I would do as she said.

After Sunday dinner I told my mom I was going to library to work on a project for school. My excuse was sufficiently specific and vague. Since I was an A student I knew she'd buy it. I peddled as fast as my legs could work the peddles on my red Huffy bicycle.

Miss Maybelle was waiting for me as I coasted into her parking lot. Since everyone in her house was up all night and slept most of the day she was just finishing her usual breakfast: a biscuit with honey and a cup of very strong, black coffee; then a Pabst Blue Ribbon beer, a Pall Mall cigarette and more coffee. This was the only time she drank alcohol and she only had one. "Gets my blood flowing. And there's a lot of me for the blood to get to," she chuckled. I quickly learned that a lit Pall Mall was always between her fingers, between her lips, or somewhere close by.

She sat in her rocker and motioned for me to sit in the swing. "What did you tell your mother?"

"I lied and said I was going to the library. I hate not telling the truth."

"Here's what I've learned about always telling the complete truth. "The truth is like a double-edged sword. You better be careful how you swing it."

She lit another cigarette from the one she was smoking. She took a deep, long drag and exhaled a thick, gray-white smoke ring that got bigger and bigger as it floated off the porch. "Tell me what you think happens in my house?"

I was not ready for her question. She was not one to beat around the bush. I felt faint again.

"Sonny, you get paid for providing a service-delivering the newspaper, right? My girls and I provide a service, too. You have customers, we have customers. You try to keep your customers happy and we do too. And sometimes, when we do, we get tipped for it just like I tip you each week." *This is starting to make some sense* I thought.

"Do you know what the service is we provide?"

I swallowed hard. "Sex." *There, I said it. I hope I don't pass out again.*

"That's true. But sex is the vehicle for many other services we provide to our customers. We also provide understanding, romance, fantasy, compassion, sympathy, warmth, and the security that comes from holding some one really close. Do you understand?"

"No ma'am."

"Every girl here has had a hard life. Most ran away from home or got kicked out. Some end up here because they didn't know what to do or where to go. Some are hiding out from men who hurt them and would again if the could. I give them a place to live that's warm and loving and safe, where they're accepted without question. Everybody knows that Miss Maybelle has powerful friends and you best not mess with her girls. Does that help any?"

"A little."

"Well, you'll understand some day." *Great, more stuff I have to wait to find out.*

At that point she began asking questions about me. For the rest of the time I told what few details there were about my meager little life. I have to say, though, I had never met a more gracious and interesting person than Miss Maybelle. We chatted for a couple of hours and then I excused myself, not wanting to bring suspicion on my subterfuge so I could use it again. As I was leaving she asked me if I would come back that she "so enjoyed" talking with me. I felt the same way.

She walked me to the steps and then said "Sonny, there are three rules for us to be friends. The first rule is under no circumstance are you allowed in my house. Besides getting me in all kinds of trouble it's not right and you have no business in there. The second rule is you never ask about me or where I get my information. The third is you never repeat to anyone anything we talk about. Do I have your word?"

"Yes ma'am." Then we shook hands and I left.

I managed to find time each week to stop by but Sunday afternoons were when we could spend the most time together. My mom never questioned my regular library visits. "Must be a really big project" she'd say as she kissed me bye and instructed me to be careful. I think she looked forward to my library visits, too. Sunday afternoon was the only time she had to herself. She worked long hours for terrible pay as a waitress. I hated that she worked as hard as she did for such little pay and the humiliation waiting tables caused her.

Listening to Miss Maybelle was a real treat. Oh, the stories she could tell. She'd confirm or refute any gossip going around town especially about prominent members of the community. I did learn the truth about Reverend Barnett. It seems that the good reverend was a regular customer making her house his last stop for Thursday night church visitation. Apparently, this went on for sometime until one Thursday night the house was disturbed by the sound of metal crashing into metal. Miss Maybelle sent Reverend Barnett out to plead with Mrs. Barnett to stop repeatedly crashing her car into his new Cadillac Sedan the church had bought him. It was all I could do to keep from telling Johnny Walker the truth.

I was always amazed that she knew the things she knew, not just about what happened in town but about everything. I never knew how long her stories would take because of the regular interruptions for more coffee or more cigarettes. Sometimes I got the feeling she didn't want me to leave. One Sunday afternoon I got up the courage to ask about Aunt Buena.

"Do you know about my Aunt Buena? Since you know pretty much everything that's happened in town, I thought you might know what happened to her? That maybe one of your special friends might have told you." She starred straight ahead.

"Everyone knows about that. She ran off to Texas with some good-for-nothing boy. After a while he beat her up, stole all her money, and abandoned her in some one horse town in the Texas panhandle."

"I wonder why she didn't try to come home?"

"She wanted to but was too ashamed and was afraid your grandfather wouldn't let her. He can be a very stubborn man, you know." I really wanted to ask her how she knew all of this.

"Do you know where she is now?

"Last I heard she had her own business of some kind and was making a lot of money." *Good for her. At least someone in the family is* I thought. "I'm not sure where she is now." I was also dying to also ask her about my father but didn't.

***

It was two weeks before Christmas. Annalee and Gladys were coming home with their new husbands, Annalee's third and Gladys' fourth. All of the Edwards girls hadn't been home for Christmas at the same time in years. They all had lived other places except me and momma; I don't think she ever lived anywhere except in our house. If she did I didn't know about it. Catherine moved back home a couple of years ago. She had married a much older man who died of lung cancer just two years after they were married. Like Catherine, he smoked several packs of Pall Malls each day.

Seems all of the members of my family did, except Ma, who dipped snuff, and momma.

Momma had a regular boyfriend who was a very kind and generous man and extremely good to all of us. He treated her like a queen, even on the occasions when she didn't deserve it. They'd have dinner together on Tuesdays, Thursdays, and Saturdays. He'd pick us up for church on Sunday and take us to dinner afterward that is if Ma hadn't cooked for everyone. They obviously loved each other but never married. He was a Catholic turned Baptist and was divorced. I don't know if my mom had ever been married. But they both agreed it was a sin for them to get married. I never understood it. *Surely God was more understanding than that* I thought when I saw them together.

Ma was beside herself with anticipation that all of her girls, except Buena of course, would be home for Christmas this year. She made Echie buy a really big tree, much bigger than we usually had. After supper each evening Momma and I spent time decorating it. This was our time when it was just she and I. Echie would be watching the *Honeymooners*, Ma would do the dishes and then rock in her room reading her Bible, and Catherine would be in her room with the door closed smoking, playing solitaire, and sipping Jack Daniels.

"Momma, may I ask you something?"

"Sure, son. What is it?"

"Since everyone else will have a friend for Christmas dinner, may I bring one, too?"

She turned her shoulders and looked at me. I had never invited anyone home before.

"Of course you can. Who is it?"

Remembering what Miss Maybelle had said about the truth I responded, "This girl who lives on my paper route." Technically, it wasn't a lie. I could see me asking my mother to bring the local madam to our house for Christmas dinner. *Yeah, that'd go over big.*

"What about her family? Won't she be having dinner with them?"

"She's older than me and doesn't have any family." Again not a lie. "I feel really sorry for her. She's really nice to me. Please, may I?"

She immediately assumed I had a crush on this older, mystery woman. But seeing how important it was to me she agreed. The next morning I set a new record that surely would go down in the paperboys' hall of fame for quickest delivery without a complaint so I could get to Miss Maybelle's and ask her. Since my visit was unscheduled I prepared to knock on the door. I saw her sitting at the kitchen table. She put a note in an envelope, sealed it, and put it in one of six shoe boxes sitting on the table. Then she put the boxes in a shopping bag and disappeared into the house. I decided not to knock. In a few minutes she came out. She bent down and kissed me on the top of my head. She'd never done anything like that before.

"You're early."

"I hurried so I could get here. I have something

really important to ask you."

She took a big sip of the awful looking stuff she called coffee and then a big drag from a Pall Mall. "Okay, Sonny Suffrage, what's on your mind?"

I took both of her hands and blurted out "Will you have Christmas dinner with me at our house?"

As soon as the words hit her ears, she spit her coffee all over both of us in one big loud choking cough. I wiped my face as she continued to cough. I was sure she'd cough up pieces of her lungs any second. When she finally caught her breath she sat in her rocker and looked dazed. "Now say that again."

"Will you have Christmas dinner with me at our house? Everyone will be there and they are all bringing someone. And I want to bring you."

"Sonny, I can't do that. It's very sweet of you to ask me but it's simply out of the question."

"Why?"

"Well, it just is."

"Christmas is when you're supposed to be with your family and friends. I know where you'll be- you'll be right here with the girls who aren't with their families. Even though people may be here you'll feel alone and you'll miss your family whoever and wherever they are. Well, I'm asking you to be a part of mine." I was getting through to her, I could tell. "Will you at least think about it? It'd mean so much to me. I've never invited anyone home before." *That ought to do it,* I thought.

She alternately gulped coffee and took big drags

on her cigarette. "I'll think about it but don't get your hopes up."

I bent down and hugged her neck. "Gotta get home. Promise you'll think hard?" I said as I bounded down the steps. She just nodded as she lit another Pall Mall.

Neither of us brought it up for several days. My mom was pressing me to finalize the dinner guest list. Then three days before Christmas Miss Maybelle sat me down on the porch swing.

"Sonny, I'll be delighted to be your guest for Christmas dinner. Let me ask you something. Does you family now who I am?"

"They know who Miss Maybelle is and what her house is if that's what you mean?"

"They may not let me stay once they realize who I am. I'm not going to make a scene but I won't be insulted. You need to understand if that happens I'll leave immediately. Okay?"

"Yes ma'am. I understand but it will be fine, you'll see. I'll put a message in the box about what time you need to be there."

"Alright but I'm not going to get there until just before dinner and I'll leave right after."

"Whatever you say," and off I went to tell momma.

***

I waited anxiously at the front door watching for Miss Maybelle's car. This was going to be the best

Christmas ever. Everyone was going to have someone special for dinner.

"Sonny, looks like she's not coming" my mom said as she put her arm around my shoulder and pulled me next to her.

"She'll be here, I know it. Just a few more minutes."

"I'm sorry, son. It's time to sit down."

I moped over to the table. Everyone was seated. I pulled my chair out.

Knock. Knock. Knock.

"It's her!" I said as I ran to the door. There was Miss Maybelle looking more beautiful than ever. She had a shopping bag; I could see several wrapped presents in it. I took her coat. She was nervous, I could tell. Then I took her by the hand.

Only a small part of the living room could be seen from the dining room. Everyone knew my mystery guest was there but no one could see who she was. The table talk got progressively less and less until all was quiet. Everyone was looking to see who'd be coming around the corner to join us for Christmas dinner.

As we appeared my mother gasped. Then all the women gasped. *Great, it didn't take long for them to figure out who she was* I thought. *At least introduce her, dummy.* My mother, my aunts, and grandparents just starred at Miss Maybelle. *Do something Sonny.*

"Everyone this is..." Before I could finish Miss Maybelle stepped toward the table and said "Merry

Christmas Ma. Merry Christmas Jocelyn and so on moving from aunt-to-aunt-to-aunt calling each by name. *This is really weird. How's she know them?*

Then she paused and looked straight at Echie.

"Merry Christmas, Papa." Time froze.

Papa? Papa? Did she call him Papa?

They all pushed their chairs back and rushed to her, each wanting to hold her and touch her trying to erase thirty years of worry and regret and guilt in that one overwhelming instant. I just stood there repeating *Papa* over and over. They were laughing and crying and kissing and hugging. This went on for several minutes.

"That's enough girls. Sit back down" Echie said with his usual lack of emotion. He hadn't even acknowledged her presence. *What now? I won't let him insult her,* I promised myself.

Echie got up and walked into the kitchen. I looked at Miss Maybelle. *She had put all of her hate, her anger, and her pride aside only to have her father respond with bitterness and contempt. It took great courage for her to come here and he smashed it just like that* I thought as I got madder and madder. I took her by the hand to walk her to the door.

"You all scoot down" Echie said to Annalee. Miss Maybelle and I turned to see Echie putting a vacant chair next to him where she always sat. "You can seat her, Sonny."

"You all stop your sniffling." I seated Miss Maybelle or Buena or whatever her name is. Then

he said "Bow your heads for the blessing."
Blessing? There's never a blessing, ever.

"Dear Lord, thank you for bringing Buena
home" he said his voice cracking and filled with
emotion. "And happy birthday, Jesus. Amen."

I kept repeating to myself *Miss Maybelle is my
Aunt Buena. My Aunt Buena owns a whore house.*
After the shock eased a little, everyone began
bombarding her with typical questions: Where you
been? What have you been doing? Are you
married? Stuff like that.

"Settle down. Settle down. There'll be plenty of
time for that" Echie said like he had done million of
times before. Then everyone began eating and
chatting just like nothing out of the ordinary had
happened.

When dinner was over everyone went into the
living room for coffee and to smoke. Miss Maybelle
(since I had never met Aunt Buena I had trouble
thinking of her other than Miss Maybelle) said she
needed to go. Everyone begged her to stay; her
sisters were dying to know about the past thirty
years.

"No, I really must be going. We can catch up
another time. But before I go I have something for
each of you." She got the shopping bag and took out
the gifts and asked me to give them out.

"I always believed I'd have the chance to give
these to you someday. I have a request; though. You
can't open them until I've gone. You'll understand
in a few minutes." As I helped her put on her coat it

hit me-*they don't know she's Miss Maybelle. They just know she lives on my paper route.*

When we got to the door she turned, smile at me, cupped my chin in her hand and simply said "thank you." At that moment we both knew she would not come back again. Then she left.

As soon as the door closed Annalee ripped the paper of her gift. There in her hands was one of the boxes I saw on Miss Maybelle's kitchen table; thirty years worth of letters and cards to each of them right there in their laps.

I went out on the porch just as she pulled away. *There goes my Aunt Buena* I thought. *She can go back to being Miss Maybelle tomorrow, but tonight she's Buena, Ester and Estes Edwards' daughter, my Aunt, and my friend.* When I went back inside everyone was thoroughly engrossed reading their letters, especially Echie.

Transforming Christmas

Transforming Christmas

He shall gather the lambs with his arms...
And gently lead those that are with young. (Isaiah
40:11)

From all indications Dr. G. M. Boyd was mean, insensitive, and cared very little, if any, for anyone else. He was not warm. He was not funny. He was not interesting. His life seemed devoid of passion and joy and excitement. G. M. Boyd was a man we thought we knew-a man we thought we understood. But we were wrong.

***

The intersection of Washington Pike and Valley View Road was quite literally the crossroads of all that happened in our neighborhood. On the corners were John H. Burkhart Elementary School, Newton's service station, Whitehead's grocery store, and G. M. Boyd Drug and Apothecary. Within a stone's throw in any direction were no fewer than six churches incorporating every protestant denomination. The Catholics and Jews were not in evidence. All the essentials of body and soul were right there at "The Corner," as we called it.

If you were a teenager in our neighborhood you were expected to have a job. Our parents believed in the life-lessons of work, lessons lost on us at the time, and that work was an important ingredient in our maturation. It was also a requirement if we wanted our own spending money, an essential part of engaging in social life and grooming our image.

All of the local merchants were good to hire neighborhood kids; there were advantages and disadvantages to working at each. The gas station paid the most but it was nasty, dirty work, and if you worked there you were known as a "greaser," a definite draw-back on the coolness scale. And you always smelled either like gasoline or Mo-Jo, the miracle hand cleaner used by mechanics world-wide. Mo-Jo looked like a yellowish thick custard that would eat through baked-on engine gunk and remove rust from cars, but it was harmless to skin. You simply dug a big wad out of the can with your fingers, rubbed it all over your hands, rinsed them off, and just like magic, they were clean.

Whitehead's grocery was a good place to work.

Most kids became bagboys or stock boys. Bagboys stayed pretty busy and got occasional tips but they had to carry out groceries in the rain and in cold weather, usually for little old ladies with pillbox hats, big coats, and one hand clutching a huge handbag large enough to carry all of their worldly possessions, and a wooden cane with a rubber tip in the other. Stock boys got to stay inside but they also had to sweep floors, dust the grocery shelves, and worst of all, track down items for customers, usually the same little old ladies, who always wanted an item no longer in stock.

Being a delivery boy at G. M. Boyd's was the coolest of all the neighborhood jobs. It also paid the least. However, its greatest advantage, the thing that overshadowed all the advantages of the other jobs and the disadvantages of working at the drug store, and the thing that gave you major cool-guy points was the delivery car-a 1965 fire engine red Camero Super Sport with a white bumble bee stripe around the rear, reverse rim hubcaps, and redline tires. It had a 327 engine and four-in-the-floor manual transmission. To us, there was no cooler car.

Delivering prescriptions and other sundries in the Camero created all manner of opportunities for coolness and mischief. You could meet friends, or your girlfriend if you had one, and let them ride with you, which of course was against the rules. You could smoke in the car and not worry too much about getting caught. However, the ultimate advantage was cruising "the Triangle"- driving among the three local drive-in hamburger joints-the Krystal, the Blue Circle, and the Orange Julius-and then start the circuit over again. Everyone who was anyone hung-out at these places and made the circuit at least five times a night. Friday nights saw an endless bumper-to-bumper ribbon of cars full of teenagers connecting all points of the Triangle. There was one very distinct disadvantage, however, to working at the drug store-Dr. G. M. Boyd, pharmacist and owner.

A product of the Great Depression and inescapable Puritan lineage, Dr. Boyd had no time for chit-chat. He was strictly business. He worked his way through college and pharmacy school and still managed to save enough money to start his own business upon acquiring his pharmacist license. "Never work for any one; only work for yourself. If you do you won't have to worry what others might be doing to your money and you" was a theme we heard frequently.

He bought an old three story house that from the front appeared to be only two stories since the basement was mostly underground and could only be seen from the side; converted the basement into a physician's office, a slick business move on his part; made the main floor into the drug store; and used the third floor as his residence. There was a detached two-car garage with an apartment behind the store. We knew of no one who had ever been upstairs or in his apartment.

If you worked for Dr. Boyd, a title employees

were required to use, you came to work on time when you were supposed to, sick or not, and you followed his rules to the letter. If you didn't, you didn't work very long. He wore one of those white "doctor" shirts that snapped across the shoulder and came up to his neck and was worn with the shirt tail out.

We knew very little about him. What we did know was mostly neighborhood stories we all accepted as truth, though who knows if they were. We didn't even know what G. M. stood for. He was matter-of-fact, cordial to customers, and gruffly interacted with and barked orders to employees, especially delivery boys. Requirements to get and stay employed at G.M. Boyd Drug and Apothecary were regular church attendance, 98% school attendance (he allowed for two absences a semester) but expected 100%, and at least a C in every course each grading period. He greatly valued education. As chintzy as he was he gave every delivery boy a quarter for each B and fifty cents for each A on his report card. Making the honor roll could subsidize dates and cruising the Triangle for a month. Most of us rarely got more than a dollar, usually fifty cents or less.

It was the car that made everyone clamor and conspire to work for Dr. Boyd. Cool wheels made the crummy hours and crummy pay and being yelled at worthwhile. Everyone who saw us in it knew it was the delivery car but no one cared. The fact they we got to drive it was enough for us and our constant quest to be cool. However, we would occasionally venture into alien domains and act as if the car were ours as we cruised other high school circuits. We never understood how such an uncool, demanding, intolerant, unsympathetic, cheap man as G. M. Boyd could have such an expensive, cool car. And let teenage boys drive it to boot. It was one of life's little mysteries.

***

Mrs. Eloise Hempstead lived on Adair Avenue within easy walking distance of the drug store, Whitehead's grocery, and Antioch Baptist Church. "I don't need a car," she was fond of saying, "I have all I need at the Corner. Besides, if the Good Lord wanted me to have a car he'd see that I had one. I can catch the bus if I need to go somewhere I can't walk to."

Miss Eloise, as we called her except when Dr. Boyd was around, came to work at the drug store not long after it opened. She was a beautiful woman and was everything he was not. Slim, fair, and fragile, she made the drudgery of working at the drug store bearable. She always wore a dress to work-no skirts, certainly no pants, always a dress that swished when she walked and swirled when she turned.

We didn't know much about her either: only where she lived and she lived alone. We thought she had been married but we weren't sure. We also knew that Dr. Boyd seemed almost like a real person when she was close by. She was able to deflect his verbal insults when one of us broke the rules and he wanted to fire us. She called us her boys. We all loved her, we couldn't help it.

The daytime delivery man was Clarence Phillips (C. P. for short) who lived in the garage apartment and was also supposed to be the watchman and grounds keeper, both of which he did only when forced. We thought he came with the house, sort of a package deal.

Clarence was tied to the mafia, that's what the neighborhood story was anyway. He'd talk of pseudo gangsters and that he could get anything we needed, even having people knocked off. It was difficult to determine truth from imagination with him because he made everything so believable. The basic facts were usually pretty accurate; it was the details that we were uncertain about.

In addition to living in the garage apartment, C. P. could also use the delivery car for important personal business and emergencies. Clarence had a much more liberal definition of "important personal business" than Dr. Boyd did. Whenever Dr. Boyd confronted him about misusing the delivery car, Clarence always apologized, begged for forgiveness, and promised, "I'll never do it again, I swear." Of course they both knew he would.

Miss Eloise and C. P. were the only full time workers. Ida Mae Stallings and Roscoe Whitaker worked part time during the peak hours everyday.

119

Little was known about them, either. Mrs. Stallings was nice enough but largely ignored everyone except Roscoe. She was more interested in reading about the latest beauty aids and trying out cosmetics than anything else.

We loved Roscoe Whitaker. He told great stories: blood-and-guts stories from the "Big War;" stories about barroom brawls, and running moonshine with the police in hot pursuit. And he didn't spare our tender ears from telling his stories with lots of very colorful language. We became his accomplices in stealing cigarettes-our attempt to "walk on the wild side." Whoever emptied the waste cans always got a wink from Roscoe when he was low on cigarettes. We'd slip a carton of Marlboros into the trash bag, take the bag to the dumpster, take out the carton, and then put it in the special hiding place for Roscoe to get later. It was a great system. If Dr. Boyd ever found out we'd get fired, not Roscoe. If we ratted him out, he'd get C. P. to have us killed! We knew it!

The atmosphere and décor of the Drug Store were clinical, no-nonsense just like its owner. The store was always open: "people get sick on holidays, too. What kind of pharmacist would I be if I let my customers down when they needed me" was his typical response. Cruddy Fowler (named for his cruddy attitude) once mentioned that people get sick in the middle of the night, too, and the store wasn't open then. Cruddy was fired on the spot. No one, and I mean no one, dared question Dr. Boyd's judgment.

Holidays would come and go unnoticed and unadorned, with two exceptions. For Memorial Day he would put out an American flag (I later learned the flag held some importance to him) and closed the store early. The other exception was Christmas.

The store closed at 5:00 p. m. on Christmas Eve and remained closed until 8:00 a. m. the day after Christmas. Even though he did nothing to celebrate Christmas, he recognized that his employees and their families did. Dr. Boyd did allow Miss Eloise and Ida Mae to decorate the store a little. He held out for years, but their persistence finally wore him down. It wasn't much: a little artificial tree on the counter by the cash register, another larger one just inside the front door, and some red and green garland strung along the counter, the boundary that separated his inner sanctum-the land of pain killers, sleeping pills, antibiotics, and all manner of other mysterious concoctions-from the rest of the store.

***

It was a Saturday, Christmas Eve. I had just finished my first delivery and one completion of the Triangle circuit. When I arrived back at the store there was an ambulance loading someone in the back. Ida Mae was crying hysterically. Roscoe had one cigarette in his mouth and one between his fingers. Clarence was pacing hurriedly along-side the ambulance as though he was hiding from someone (like the police). Miss Eloise stood holding one of the ambulance doors.

Ida Mae ran up to me as I crossed the parking lot. She grabbed me, her newly applied Christmas Rose eye shadow running down her cheeks and mixing with her "Barely There" pink rouge, and squeezed me until my breath was gone. "It's Dr. Boyd, he's dead!" She screamed in between heaving sobs.

Her message of death shot straight through me. I'd never seen a dead person before.

"He's not dead, Ida Mae, at least not yet" Miss Eloise said calmly but authoritatively. "Roscoe, take Ida Mae back inside. Clarence, you go too. Benjie, you stay here with me."

As the ambulance pulled away, Miss Eloise turned to me. "How late can you work?"

"As long as you need me to." All of the delivery boys would do anything for Miss Eloise.

"We're going back in and I'm going to talk to everyone. Then I need you to take me to the hospital."

"Yes ma'am. Anything you want, Miss Eloise, anything."

I opened the door for Miss Eloise and we went in. She gathered everyone in the back of the store like a mother hen gathering her brood. Since I already had my instructions I remained available to assist customers. Her instructions were clear; we would all pull together and do whatever we had to do to help G. M. (she was the only one who could call him that) in his gravest hour. And that meant keeping the store open and functioning just as if he were there. Clarence, Ida Mae, and Roscoe would assist customers and take orders. She'd be back shortly.

"Let's go."

"Yes, ma'am."

Fortunately, the hospital was close by, so there weren't long uncomfortable pauses in conversations.

"He's not like you think. He's very warm and gentle," Miss Eloise said, fighting back tears.

Excuse me? Are we talking about the same Dr. G. M. Boyd? The one who yells at the his employees, especially the delivery boys? The one with no kindness at all for others? The one who would ignore Christmas if you'd let him? I thought but didn't say.

"He really is a very kind, sweet man."

Miss Eloise have you been in the narcotics cabinet or something? "Yes ma'am."

By now we were at the emergency room entrance. She reached over placed her hand on mine, and said, "I'm counting on you Benjie. I'll call you in a little while and have you come get me, okay?"

"Yes, ma'am. I'll be waiting. Don't worry, Miss Eloise, it'll be all right"

Then she passed me a dull gold key. "This is the master key. I need for you to go up to the third floor and go to his desk. It's in his study, the first room to the right. The desk key is under the rug under the

123

desk chair. Unlock the roll-top and push it back. In the bottom left-hand drawer you'll find some files. One will be labeled 'Will and Power of Attorney.' Get it and bring it to me when you pick me up."

"Yes, ma'am."

"Benjie, you have to promise that you'll go directly to the desk, get the file, and leave immediately. You won't look around. And you won't read the papers in the file. Promise!"

"I promise." Then she shut the door and went inside, not knowing what she'd find.

I now had a dilemma. I had the opportunity to go where none of us thought we'd ever have the chance to go, into Dr. Boyd's house. We'd wondered and speculated what it must look like: bare walls, dim lighting, everything very neat and in its place, no books, no pictures of family or friends, nothing interesting at all. But the promise to Miss Eloise was significant. If I had made it to any one other than Miss Eloise I would have certainly conducted a thorough inspection of his house without thinking twice. But promising Miss Eloise was different, especially under the circumstances.

Just as I passed John H. Burkhart Elementary School and in between Elvis' "Blue Christmas" and Johnny Mathis' "The Christmas Song" on the radio, it hit me. "She's his girlfriend. Miss Eloise is Dr. Boyd's sweetheart. Why else would she defend him like that? How else would she know where his will was and have a key to the third floor? She takes care of him. It makes perfect sense," I said out loud.

All bets were off now. I checked in with Ida Mae and Roscoe. Clarence was at his house Lord knows doing what. The last minute rush hadn't hit yet. Ida Mae had removed and re-applied her eye shadow (Cinnamon was the new shade) and seemed in control. After I covered for Roscoe while he chain-smoked several Marlboros outside, I went to the back of the store next to the refrigerator and stood looking at the door that led upstairs to the private, personal domain of Dr. G. M. Boyd, the pharmacist with a secret life. *Sorry Miss Eloise, he deserves it,* I thought as I unlocked the door.

It was nothing like I expected. The rooms were bright and airy. The walls were painted in warm earth tones. Several abstract paintings and classic prints matching the room's decor were perfectly hung. The furniture was a combination of early American and primitive antiques. A large console television was in the living room, his recliner placed directly in front. The kitchen had all of the modern appliances. A few dishes were stacked in the sink. In the middle of his bedroom was an antique brass bed with fancy scroll work in the headboard. There was a chair and footstool in front of the window. Several books were stacked on the night stand and the table beside the chair. His closet was full of bright sport shirts, pastel dress shirts, lots of boldly colored ties, and a number of expensive suits and sport coats. *I must be in the Twilight Zone. The guy I work for can't possibly live here.*

After my brief inventory of his house I went

into the study. I was amazed at what I saw. Two walls were floor-to-ceiling bookshelves filled with all manner of books-classics, history, do-it-yourself, bestsellers, biographies, theology, art, you name it. It was a veritable library. In one corner was a cupboard that also reached from floor to ceiling. In it was expensive stereo equipment; four large speakers were strategically placed throughout his study. At the bottom of the cupboard were two rows of phonograph albums-Frank Sinatra, Miles Davis, Glenn Miller, Bob Dylan, the Beatles, Bill Monroe, and lots of classical artists, especially Mozart, were among the selections.

Next to the desk was an antique writing table. File folders were stacked on one side, a writing tablet was in the middle; papers in no apparent order were stacked on the other side. Right in the center, next to the back edge of the table was a picture of a beautiful young woman who obviously was Miss Eloise. *I knew it!* Then I turned my attention to the desk and completing my mission.

I unlocked the desk and pushed the roll top up. Stuff was crammed into every one of the little cubby holes. A souvenir cup from Yankee Stadium held pens and pencils. I sat down in the swivel chair and pulled open the bottom left drawer. It was crammed with folders. As I began searching for the will and power of attorney file, I noticed files whose labels were familiar: Clarence Phillips, Eloise's Mortgage, 1965 Camero, Ida Mae Stallings, and Roscoe Whitaker.

I didn't want to spend too much time in Dr. Boyd's house. Heaven forbid that anyone would find out that I broke my promise to Miss Eloise. I pulled out the folder and opened it on the desk. *Ah, Ha! Just as I thought.* The name Eloise P. Hempstead prominently appeared in several places on both documents. I closed the folder and hurried back downstairs, thinking *I've gotta look some more. This is unbelievable.*

Business had been steady. We all wondered if Dr. Boyd was still alive and if so how he was doing. While I was more worried about Miss Eloise but given what I found out I was a little worried about Dr. Boyd now. I stationed myself close to the front door to act as doorman. About noon Miss Eloise called. She updated everyone through Ida Mae. Then she asked to speak to me.

"Benjie, did you find the folder?"

"Yes, ma'am."

"Did you look in it?"

"No ma'am," I said with some inflection in my voice. I hated lying to her but I hated disappointing her more.

"G. M. has had a stroke. It's serious but the doctors think he'll be okay. He'll have to take it easy for a while. He can't move his legs, only barely move his arms, and he can't talk. They seem to think that he'll recover though. I'm going to stay here a little longer. I need to get back to the store. Pick me up in an hour."

"Yes ma'am, I'll be there."

"Thank you, Benjie."

An hour! I didn't have much time. A quick survey revealed that the store was in good hands. Back to Dr. Boyd's I went.

I sat down in the swivel desk chair and pulled open the bottom drawer. I quickly found the folders with the familiar names and started with the one labeled "Eloise's mortgage." It quickly became clear that Dr. Boyd bought her the house and made the mortgage payment for years until he had paid it off. There was a bill of sale from him to her for the house in the amount of one hundred dollars. *He sold her the house for a hundred bucks. This is very strange.* There was no more information in the file.

Then I pulled out the file marked 1965 Camero. This would tell the story, the one we had all wondered about. As I looked through the documentation I was amazed. Dr. Boyd had bought the car from Eloise Hempstead. *Why would Miss Eloise have a car? She can't drive,* I thought out loud. Other documentation clearly indicated the bank was about to repossess the car. Then I found a newspaper article whose headline read, "Teenager's Death Ruled Accidental." It was about some kid named Eric Slover who was killed in a shooting incident.

There was a picture of Miss Eloise and a teenage boy leaning against the car with the inscription at the bottom: "Eric and Eloise, Eric's first car." It didn't make sense. *Is the boy her son and if he is who's his father? Is it Dr. Boyd? I wonder if he got her pregnant and took care of them out of guilt. Then when the boy died he took over the car for the deliveries. He probably bribed her with the house to keep her quiet about him being the father. Of course the jerk wouldn't marry her.* I felt no pity for him any more. *Poor Miss Eloise. She must really love him to still take care of him* I thought.

However, the more I looked the more it became abundantly clear my assessment of Dr. Boyd was completely wrong. It seems he gave Ida Mae Stallings a job to keep her out of jail. She was a petty thief and had been arrested several times. If she was arrested again she'd be sent to prison for the rest of her life for being a habitual criminal. The City Judge, who felt sorry for Ida Mae, called Dr. Boyd and asked if he'd help her out. Dr. Boyd gave her a job, helped her find a place to live, and basically start a new life. She hasn't been in trouble since.

Roscoe Whitaker is a recovering alcoholic Dr. Boyd took under his wing. Roscoe was found quite literally in the gutter passed out drunk by the police. Apparently the police know they can count on Dr. Boyd to help out with problems that require creative solutions. Like Ida Mae, Dr. Boyd helped Roscoe dry out, let him live with Clarence for free until he got on his feet, helped him qualify for financial assistance from the government, and gave him a job. Although he smokes three packs of Marlboros a day he hasn't had a drop to drink in seven years.

Clarence had been convicted of dealing drugs, being a Peeping Tom, and as he would say, "distributing adult art works and educational aides." Unfortunately, at one time Clarence delivered for some very unsavory characters who would now like to help him meet his maker. As it turns out, Clarence was, indeed, associated with the local crime bosses. Dr. Boyd's minister got word of Clarence, who was being booted out of his half-way house for violating house rules. Without a place to go that was unknown to his former colleagues his life would be in danger. The minister immediately called Dr. Boyd who rescued Clarence, too.

At the back of the drawer were four notebook-sized ledger books labeled Prescriptions, Loans, Rent & Utilities, and Miscellaneous. Each book contained literally hundreds of names with notations explaining what each was. None had ever been repaid. I saw some names I knew in each of them but spent little time reading them. "I wonder what treasures the other drawers will yield," I said out loud.

In the bottom right drawer were three medium sized boxes labeled Notes, Christmas Cards, and Pictures. The notes were thank you notes for paying someone's rent, for medicine he gave for free, for working out free medical treatment from Dr. Goovus downstairs, and on and on. The same applied to the Christmas card box. Apparently, these were his favorite; some went back to when he first opened the store. Like the ledger books, both boxes had hundreds of cards. The pictures were mostly of Eloise. A few were of what appeared to be college buddies. There was one picture of him and Eloise when they were much younger.

In with the pictures was an opened envelope that proved how really badly I had pieced the puzzle of Dr. Boyd's life together. The letter was from Miss Eloise. I glanced at it but quickly stopped-it was just too personal. I read enough to see she was thanking him for his offer to marry her and raise her child as his own but he wasn't the father and she didn't love him. And she wasn't going to marry someone she didn't love. *Why would he keep a letter that must have broken his heart?*

I sat there taking it all in. The man we despised had been giving out free medicine, paying rent and bills for others, taking in people who society had discarded, arranging free medical care, and using his influence solely for helping others all of his life and doing it without any acknowledgement or recognition; doing it just because it was the right thing and because he could.

I quickly put everything back in its place, hurried down the stairs, ran out and hopped in the car, and sped off to get Miss Eloise. I pulled up right as she walked out. *Whew, that was close.* I knew I would have no believable excuse for being late.

"How is he?" She looked surprised. She knew we all hated him and only worked there to drive the car.

"He's still in very serious condition. There's nothing we can do except pray and wait."

131

Once back at the drug store Miss Eloise filled several prescriptions for life-sustaining drugs so our customers wouldn't be without them on Christmas. If the truth were known she had probably filled prescriptions on other occasions. She sent everyone home. I made the final deliveries and then took her back to the hospital.

We were almost back at the hospital when she said, "Oh Benjie, I forgot to turn on the alarm. We need to go back."

"Miss Eloise, I know how to do it. I can go by on my way home."

"Would you? That would be really wonderful."

"Consider it done." My act of kindness was partially motivated by my desire to go back upstairs. There was something I needed to confirm.

"Benjie, drive the car to your house. I don't want it there for Clarence to use. Could you pick me up tomorrow, as long as it doesn't interfere with your family's plans?"

"Yes, ma'am. I'm sure it will be fine with my mom. I called her and told her what was going on."

I went around the car and helped her out. She hugged me tightly and then went back inside. I jumped in the car and hurried back to the drug store.

Once back upstairs I pulled out the box marked Pictures and took out the letter again. It was dated December 24th. Miss Eloise told him that since she was pregnant with another man's child she couldn't have dinner with him that night, and she was very sorry for any pain she caused him. I just sat there. My opinion of Miss Eloise hadn't changed; my opinion of him had. As I put the box back I noticed something in the back corner of the drawer. It was a small, black velvet box. I opened it and found a fairly large diamond ring, obviously an engagement ring. *He was going to ask her to marry him at dinner the Christmas Eve she gave him the letter. Wow! I'd turn mean and hate everybody, too.* Now I really felt sorry for him.

I sat there for a while longer. Then went back downstairs, turned on the alarm, locked up, and went home to whatever was left of Christmas Eve at our house. However, I couldn't get what I knew off my mind. Questions remained. Why didn't he ask her again, and if he did, why hadn't she said yes? She obviously loved him, even though she told him in the letter she didn't. And he still loved her. There was also something about her son's death that wasn't clear either.

I wanted to do something but I didn't know what. About three o'clock, as I lay in bed staring at the ceiling, it came to me. *That'll work. That's what I'll do* and then promptly went to sleep.

***

The door of Dr. Boyd's room was partially open. I could partially see Dr. Boyd's legs outlined under the sheets of his hospital bed. Miss Eloise was sitting in a chair next to his bed. I knocked and then went in.

"Morning and Merry Christmas, Miss Eloise, Dr. Boyd."

"Merry Christmas to you, Benjie."

Dr. Boyd was awake but still couldn't move his limbs or talk. He sort of blinked his eyes to acknowledge my presence.

"Did you get any sleep?" I asked Miss Eloise.

"Not much. What I could use is a cup of coffee."

"Why don't you go down to the cafeteria and get some and get out of this room for a few minutes. I'll sit with him."

"Are you sure?"

"Yes ma'am, I'm sure."

She took Dr. Boyd's hand and said "I'll just be a minute."

Convincing her to leave was central to my plan. When I was sure she was gone, I went over to Dr. Boyd and took his hand.

"Dr. Boyd, I have to tell you something, something you won't like and will probably fire me over. If you do, then you do." I took a deep breath. "I know about the Christmas Eve letter. I now you were going to take her to dinner and ask her to marry you (I was still kind of guessing but felt confident I was right this time). How I know is not important, at least not now. What is important is that you give Miss Eloise this." I slipped something in his hand.

At first he looked surprised but not angry. Then the corners of his mouth turned up a little as though he was trying to smile. "Give it to her. She loves you desperately-I think she always has. Don't worry, I'll never breath a word of what I know."

I could hear her coming down the hall. "Merry Christmas, Dr. Boyd." Then he whispered, "Merry Christmas, Benjie."

"Miss Eloise, I just came by to see how you both were doing. When you're ready to leave just call my house." Then I kissed her on the cheek and whispered, "He has something for you in his hand," and then I left. Within a few seconds I heard her exclaim, "Oh, G. M.!"

***

The morning after Christmas everyone was waiting at the front door because I had the keys. I opened the door and hurried in to turn off the alarm. Miss Eloise asked everyone to gather at the counter. She gave an update on Dr. Boyd's condition. He could move all of his limbs, he could sit up, and he could talk slowly. "It's a miracle," Roscoe said.

"Yes, a Christmas miracle" she replied. "And there's something else." Then she stuck out her arm, bent her left hand down, and there it was, sparkling like the Christmas star.

Miss Eloise looked at me and smiled. And we both knew that life at G. M. Boyd Drug and Apothecary would never be the same.

Full Circle

Full Circle

The people who walked in darkness have seen a great light. (Isaiah 9:2)

I hadn't been back in many years. There are lots of reasons-too busy, too important, too lazy, too lost, too ashamed-but none of them good enough. I thought of them everyday if only when I asked God to bless those I loved when I said my prayers. Oh, there was the usual Christmas card and a quick note here and there but nothing worthy of their constant and abiding support and love. Now I was going back to bless a granddaughter and bury her grandfather although I didn't know it at the time. And it would be on Christmas Eve.

As we cruised through the night sky I looked out the window at all the flickering lights below. From thirty thousand feet the east coast looked like giant balls of light connected by skinny strands. While my adult life had been in the light of the biggest cities it began where the light didn't shine as far.

How did I get so far from home and so lost I thought? *I had everything: the respect of my peers and the admiration of my friends; I was known throughout the country and parts of the world; I had fame and riches and whatever I wanted. And then I lost it all. How did I get so far from where I started?* My discourse with myself led me back to where and how it all began.

***

I was the first of many things in my family: the first to go to college, the first to get a job that didn't require manual labor, the first to get divorced, the first and only one to leave home. I was also the biggest source of disappointment to my parents.

We lived in Blaine, Tennessee, a small, rural community where everyone worked hard, usually farming of some kind; where you didn't have to lock your doors; and where everyone knew everyone. Blaine was close enough to Knoxville, a medium sized city, where we could find the trappings of the "big city" but still far enough away that it remained out of reach of urban sprawl.

There are six kids in my family. Ritchie, a brick mason just like our dad, is the oldest. He had no choice about his vocation. He is also a drunk, not an alcoholic, a drunk. Ronnie is a plumber and apparently not a very good one because he is always getting fired. He had been a drunk but is now a recovering alcoholic. The third in line is Rufus who spent all of his twenties in Brushy Mountain Maximum Security Prison for vehicular homicide. Insanely jealous, when he was eighteen he saw his girlfriend in a car with another boy. She tried to explain the boy was her cousin. Rufus didn't buy it. Tracked the guy down, repeatedly rammed the boy's car with our father's one and a half ton truck, and killed him. Turns out he was her cousin.

The two girls, Althea and Sophie, are next. They are both nurses' aids. Having had lots of practice stitching up their older brothers, it was a natural career choice. They never did anything remotely out of line. I'm the baby. The biggest difference in age between any of us is two years. My mother must have been pregnant for most of her young adult life.

My mother tried to get my brothers to enter the ministry. None of them did. Although Althea's and Sophie's gender prevented them from being preachers they were expected to do ministry type work. I was the one to fulfill my mother's dream.

My parents named me after Hubert Longmire, the preacher who had been at our church most of their lives. I hated it. My family called me Hubie. I liked Bert. The good reverend told my folks that if they'd name me after him he'd buy them a new baby bed. They did but he didn't. Since she almost died delivering me, momma realized I'd be the last child. I'm sure she thought that naming me as they did would increase the odds of me being a preacher.

I don't know if I actually felt the call or if I really just wanted to please my mother. At the age of twelve, a very appropriate age to begin ministering I thought, I stood up as soon as our little choir started the invitation hymn, marched confidently down the center aisle at the First Pentecostal Church, and publicly professed I was going to be a minister (preacher was too unsophisticated for me). I hadn't told anyone. My mother beamed. "Oh Hubie, Oh, Hubie, you've made my dream come true," I could hear her say from her regular seat on the third pew. And I had.

From that moment everything I did was directed toward serving God. As far as my parents were concerned the only way to truly serve the Lord was from the pulpit. I was at church every time the doors were open. I volunteered to pray during Sunday school. I read my Bible several times everyday. I regularly visited the sick and the shut-ins. If it had anything to do with spreading the Word, I did it. I studied hard in high school so I could go to college.

I received a full scholarship to Carson-Newman College, a first-rate Baptist school just down the road which thrilled my mother beyond description. When I graduated from Southern Baptist Theological Seminary, her excitement and pride were immeasurable. During my time at Carson-Newman and Southern I'd fill in for local pastors. I loved the one-on-one ministering. I didn't like preaching much at all. I wasn't sure why.

When I graduated from seminary, based on a recommendation from the Dean, I was immediately "called" to serve at the Peach Grove Baptist Church in Cannons Campground, South Carolina, just outside of Spartanburg. My first Sunday in the pulpit brought my entire family and several of our neighbors to Peach Grove Baptist Church. They filled four pews. I tried not looking at them. Every time I did my brother Ronnie would pick his nose and act like he was wiping his finger on his tie. So, I preached to the framed poster of John 3:16 next to the sanctuary doors in the back.

During the invitation hymn, the alter call to some, Joey Gordon, who was thirteen and bigger than me, joined the church. My mother was convinced my message brought the boy to the Lord. However, it was prearranged with the former pastor. I never told my mother otherwise. His baptism would be a sign.

Peach Grove Baptist was like most Baptist churches. The pews faced the pulpit platform where the Word was imparted to the congregation. Behind the platform was the choir loft and behind the choir loft was the baptistery, a pool with a glass front where your sins were washed away by being immersed in the water. The baptistery was raised several feet above the last row of the choir.

The following Sunday morning, while the congregation was singing the first hymn, I explained to Joey what would happen. He said he understood. "Are you scared?" I asked him.

"Yes sir, a little." I could tell it was more than little.

"It'll be fine. Nothing to it." This was my first, too. I was petrified.

When the hymn was over I wadded into the baptistery, my white baptismal robe floating on top of the water at first. I stood on a board that ran from side-to-side under the water. Under my robe I wore hip boots that actually came almost to my arm pits. I read about John the Baptist baptizing Jesus, said a few words about the symbolism of the sacrament, and then motioned for Joey to wade out to join me.

I placed one hand on the back of his neck, held up my other hand, and said "I baptize you, Joey Gordon, in the name of the Father, the Son, and the Holy Spirit." I had him grip my forearm with both hands and then put my hand over his nose and mouth and began to lower him into the water. Joey failed to tell me he was afraid of water.

Just as the water reached his neck he panicked and began flailing his arms. He grabbed me as if he were drowning. I slipped off the board and down we went. We rolled over and over in the water like alligators with their prey. Arms slapped the water, feet went up in the air, and still we wrestled, splashing water all over the choir who jumped up and ran out of the choir loft.

By this time my boots had filled with water which made it even more difficult to get control of

Joey. This went on for several seconds. I thought we'd both drown right there during Holy Baptism. Then with a big, loud groan and a giant push, which created a huge wave that splashed over the glass and reached all the way to the pulpit, I managed to get Joey out of the baptistery. He just lay on the steps gasping for breath like a giant carp on the river bank.

I stood up and leaned on the front glass of the Baptistery to catch my breath. Apparently all of the waves crashing against the glass put too much pressure on the seals at the bottom. Out it popped and what water was left went rushing through the choir loft, across the platform, and into the front of the sanctuary. I looked down at the flooded choir loft and platform and then out at the congregation, who sat stunned not knowing whether to laugh, cry, or fall on the knees and pray. I felt like singing a verse of *On Jordon's Stormy Bank I Stand* but thought better of it.

Not knowing what else to do I raised both arms and simply said, "Amen. Go in peace and God be with you," and sloshed my way out of the baptistery. Joey's baptism cost the church about two thousand dollars to dry and replace some of the carpet. The incident followed me the rest of my life.

The people at Peach Grove were wonderful to me. However, it became abundantly clear very quickly I was not the preacher type. I loved the people and ministering to their needs on a personal level, and I truly loved the study and preparation. I simply hated preaching. I daily asked God to make me a better preacher. It also didn't take long for that prayer to be answered.

"Bert, me and Charlie would like to take you to lunch one day this week, if you're available," Bud Anderson asked me one Sunday after the service. Bud was the head of the deacons and his brother, Charlie, was head of the finance committee. The Andersons were not just pillars of the church but of the community-their family helped found both. When one of them asked you to do something, you did it.

"Mr. Anderson, it'd be a real pleasure to meet you for lunch." Out of respect for them and the contributions they had made to the church I never called them by their first names. This luncheon meeting would clarify my uncertain future as a preacher of the gospel.

As we were having coffee after lunch Bud began, "Bert, I think your talents might lie someplace other than preaching." Then Charlie interrupted. "Son, let's get straight to the point."

I nodded up and down, caught off guard by there comments.

"Son, the fact is you can't preacher. You're great at the personal things, just not delivering the Word." Charlie was a retired Marine Colonel who had served in combat in WWII and Korea. While he was not insensitive in any way, he spoke his mind in a few words.

Bud, ever the diplomat, picked up the

conversation. "We really like you, Bert. We think of you as one of our own. How you interact with everyone on a personal basis is better than I've ever seen. When there's a crisis you're at you best. You have a real gift."

"It's just not preaching," Charlie interrupted again.

"Alright, Charlie, you've made your point. Don't jump on the boy."

"Mr. Anderson, its okay," I said to Bud. "And Mr. Anderson," I said to Charlie, "You're absolutely right. I've agonized and prayed about it for months." I caught them both by surprise with my candid admission. We all took a deep breath and had some more coffee.

"Bert, do you have any idea of what you might do besides preaching?" Bud inquired.

"It's ministering to individuals that I seem to do best and really enjoy. And I love studying and doing research."

"Have you thought about going back to school?" Bud asked with genuine interest.

"Mr. Anderson, I'd really love to go back to seminary and get a doctorate in theology, maybe in psychology but there are a few problems. I don't have the money for living expenses much less to pay tuition. And it would break my mother's heart. To her I'd be leaving the ministry. She'd be devastated."

Charlie looked at Bud then at me. "Don't worry about the money. We'll see to that. We can't help

147

you with your mother."

"I couldn't let you do that."

"Bert, as well thought of as you are in these parts I'm sure we'll have no trouble getting folks to help out. Now, what you need to do is think about it long and hard. And if this is what you truly want to do, then I feel sure it'll happen. When we put our minds to it, we can do some pretty amazing things" Bud said with real conviction.

"How much we talking about, just so we'll know where we stand?" Charlie asked. He could always be counted on to get straight to the point.

"It largely depends on where I'd go. Southern, where I went before, would be about ten thousand, not counting living expenses."

"Is that where would you like to go?" Bud asked.

"I'd love to go to Union Theological Seminary in New York. World renowned theologians, such as Dietrich Bonhoeffer, Raymond Brown, and Paul Tillich, have taught there. I've read a few of their books, especially Dr. Tillich's."

"What's Union cost?" It was clear why Charlie was chairman of the Finance Committee.

"Counting living expenses, modest living mind you, tuition, books and fees, I'd say it'd take about thirty thousand a year." I waited for one of them to gasp and say, "sorry Bert, there's no way." but neither did.

"Okay, you find out how to apply at Union Seminary, what it will cost, and we'll get back together," Bud said bringing his coffee cup to his lips as if we were talking about the weather.

"Mr. Anderson…"

"Son, seems to me you haven't quite grasped what's going on here. You're only duty is to get information. That's it. And figure out what to do about your mother. Bud and I have made up our minds. Anything unclear about that?" Charlie asked with a rye smile.

"No sir."

"Okay, then. We're all set. We need to get a move on," Charlie said as if he'd just finished briefing his Marine staff. "We'll get together same time next week." Bud and I both nodded. And we were done.

As I drove back to the church I felt like I had just had an out-of-body experience of some kind. The two most important and influential members of Peach Grove Baptist Church had told me I was a terrible preacher, and in the same breath agreed to raise enough money to send me back to seminary. *That's the strangest conversation I believe I've ever had.*

At our next lunch my going to Union Seminary had been irrevocably set in motion. For tax purposes they had established a non-profit foundation, the Anderson Foundation, which to my amazement already had eight thousand dollars. The Board members were Bud, Charlie, Bud's wife, Judy, their brother, Paul, and their sister, Creole. Bud said that with Judy and Creole on the Board there would never be any question about "where every dime came from or where every dime went."

I had done my assignment and had all the requirements for admission, tuition and fees, deadlines, and anything else that might be remotely associated with attending Union Theological Seminary. I was visibly moved by their efforts to do this for me.

"Mr. Anderson, I can't believe people have given money to help me go back to school. Why would they do that? Outside of Peach Grove no one knows me that well?"

"Bert, you'd be surprised how well known you are. Good work travels fast. People know how great you are to minister to anyone who needs it. While you may not be able to deliver them very well, you have great ideas that have inspired a lot people not just in Cannons Campground but in Spartanburg, too," Bud said.

"You know us and we know everybody," Charlie added bringing the conversation back to its lowest common denominator. "I talked to the Dean of Admissions and explained what a fine young man you are and that you'd make a top-notch theologian. After I explained a few other things to her she said she was sure there'd be no problem with your acceptance."

I'd have loved to have heard that conversation I thought.

"In case you hadn't guessed, Charlie can be very persuasive." *No kidding.*

They were both pleased I had gotten all the information and had already completed the application.

"Since both of you hold important positions in the church and community will you write recommendation letters for me?"

"Don't need any," Charlie said matter-of-factly.

"But the application clearly says…"

"Son," was all Charlie needed to say and I shut up.

Bud put his hand on my shoulder. "Bert, don't worry. We've got everything under control. Trust me. It'll be fine." From that point on and for the rest of my life I never questioned anything either of them said. They were men of their word and that was all I needed. Little did I know how much they would influence my life.

It wasn't but a few weeks until I received my acceptance letter from Union Theological Seminary. I immediately called the Andersons. Even though it was a foregone conclusion they were as excited as if I had been one of their children. We agreed to meet for lunch again and plan my departure from Peach Grove.

I announced my resignation to the congregation six weeks before I had to be at Union. This would give me enough time to take care of things at Cannons Campground, find a place to live in New York, and go home and break the news, and my mother's heart, to my family. This also allowed members of the congregation to make a donation to the Anderson Foundation in my behalf, at least that's what Charlie said.

It was time to go before I knew it. Bud and Judy invited me for dinner at their house. Of course all of the Andersons were there. As we were sitting at the table chatting after dinner, Bud asked everyone to be quiet.

"Bert, Charlie has a little something for you. But before he gives it to you I want to say something. You have touched all of our hearts and lives more than I could possibly tell you. You're one of the most genuine and giving people we've ever met. We all love you; you're a member of our family, and you're always welcome here."

I was about to cry. Judy was.

"Son, what I'm about to do gives me great pleasure, more than I thought it would. I'm proud of you," Charlie's voice cracked as he spoke. Then he gave me an envelope. In it was a cashier check for sixty thousand dollars. *Sixty thousand dollars*. Then I fell apart.

Charlie couldn't talk so Bud took over. "That ought to get you through the first two years. By then you'll know how much you'll need to finish up."

***

My decision to go back to seminary was received as I expected by my mother. I took the cowards way out and delivered the news by phone, something I'm still ashamed of. As my father related to me, "she took to her bed and stayed there for three day and did nothing but cry." When she and I finally spoke my first semester at Union Theological Seminary was almost over. She simply couldn't grasp that there were many ways to minister to people besides preaching. We never talked about it again.

I found a home at Union. I was challenged and my beliefs were challenged. Nothing escaped the toughest intellectual scrutiny. I studied under some of the pre-imminent theologians and scholars and became a disciple of Paul Tillich's brand of existentialism. I regularly found myself thinking *I bet the good folks at Peach Grove and First Pentecostal would think I'm a heretic.* However, not only was I making a name for myself in theological circles, the acclaim and notoriety created in me a much inflated sense of self-importance and arrogance that bordered on complete narcissism.

I had distinguished myself so much that upon completing my doctorate I was offered a professorship at Union, a feat unheard of for its own graduates. Of course my appointment made me almost unbearable to be around. I had my own disciples who hung on my every word. Some of my female students regularly invited me for romantic interludes. On a few occasions I accepted, knowing it was against the rules. *I'm too smart to get caught and even if I do they wouldn't dare fire me* I thought. When I did get caught and was fired I rationalized *who needs them. I'm a bestselling author known all over the country. I've outgrown Union, anyway.* Imagine, outgrowing one of the most prestigious seminaries in the world.

The years that followed saw me ruin two marriages, make and lose two fortunes, be the center of public embarrassment and humiliation, and follow in my older brothers' footsteps. My addiction wasn't alcohol-it was cocaine, an insidious white powder that seduced me and fed my cosmic ego. When it had me completely in its clutches, it destroyed me and anyone who dared try to help me.

Before I hit bottom and lost everything I had managed not only to repay the Anderson Foundation but contribute over a million dollars to do with as Bud and Charlie and the others saw fit. I paid off all family's debts. I established college funds for my nieces and nephews, and a living trust for my folks so they could enjoy life in ways they'd never been able to. I even managed to get Rufus out of jail thanks to one of my big-time New York lawyer friends. Ironically, when I really needed money, there was none to be found. My friends all seemed to be in financial straights at the same time. Imagine that.

My fall from grace ended with a very loud thud. I was arrested in a sting operation aimed at New York's elite drug addicts. I spent a few nights in jail and twenty eight days in rehab. The latter was a good will gesture by my publisher before he washed his hands of me, which he should have done long before. He, like everyone else, kept hoping I'd get straighten out and return to my bestselling form again.

It was the jail time that did it, even though it wasn't but a few days. Watching other addicts puke and wretch their guts out; being surrounded by vicious, desperate people watching me, sizing me up with their gaunt, wrinkled, lifeless faces, probably to do me harm for my clothes and watch, was a mirror of what I'd become. For the first time in years I saw my reflection clearly. I hated what I saw. They were no different than me except they were at least honest with themselves about what they were. All of us in that cell had made bad choices that led us to betray our friends, betray our families, and worst of all betray ourselves.

There, in that insect infested, urine drenched cell the shame and guilt and remorse for what my life and I had become overwhelmed me. I sat in the corner among my many smelly, ragged, end-of-their-rope look-alikes and wept bitterly, asking God for forgiveness, strength, and grace even though I deserved none.

Through it all Bud and Charlie and their families never deserted me. They knew about everything-the women, the drugs, getting fired, everything-and never mentioned it. It was uncanny; no matter where I was they always knew how to reach me. Just at the worst moments one of them would call or send a note. They were always the same: you're always welcome with us, just have faith and trust and things will be alright, we love you, call collect anytime. When I got out of rehab Bud and Charlie were waiting for me. They came all the way from Cannons Campground just to be sure I had a safe place to go. And they were armed with Judy's home cooking.

After they dropped me off Bud hugged me and said, "We all lose our way. Some of us find our way back. You're one of the lucky one."

Charlie handed me an envelope that read "Anderson Foundation" in the corner. "Here son. Whatever you need it for." Then he hugged me, too, and they left. It was the longest time before I was able to open the envelope, which contained ten thousand dollars.

That very afternoon I received a call from the Dean of Brooklyn College. He wanted to see me. He had received a call from the trustees of the Anderson Foundation, now a well known and well respected organization that helped others realize their full potential. They suggested that having a bestselling author and noted scholar and theologian on the faculty might be something Brooklyn College would benefit from, especially since they were willing to endow a chair in the Religious Studies Department. It may have been the potential endowment that cancelled out my recent infamous behavior. The Dean wasted no time calling.

"They called it the Prodigal Chair. Does that mean anything to you?" he asked with some confusion.

"Yes sir. It does." In a matter of a few days I was an Assistant Professor at Brooklyn College.

My new life and lifestyle were a far cry from my former New York life. My one bedroom apartment in Brooklyn was a little bigger than the bathroom in my previous Eastside apartment. But I was perfectly happy and felt like I was making a contribution beyond myself. I had a new book accepted by my old publisher who was certain it would far surpass the others. It was titled *Sermons I Should Have Heard but Never Did*. Ninety percent of my royalties were to be sent to the Anderson Foundation.

***

The tires screeched as they hit the runway and jolted me back from reliving how I got to where I am now. It was a terrible journey from then to now but I wouldn't change any of it, except for sparing the innocent by-standers.

Bud was waiting just inside the gate. I hurried to hug him.

"It's good to see you. Where's Charlie?" I don't think I had ever seen them apart.

"Bert, Charlie's really sick. He has advanced pancreatic cancer. He doesn't have much longer, probably just a few days."

Nothing Bud could have said would have numbed me more.

"I'll tell you about it later. First things first.

How are you doing?"

First things First? You want to know about me first?

"I'm doing just fine," was about all I could say.

On the drive into town Bud explained about Charlie. It was discovered about two months ago, that it was inoperable, and Charlie was in a lot of pain and stayed sedated most of the time. He was at Bud's house. "Don't let me die in no damn hospital" were his instructions to Bud.

"You want to go by and see him?"

"Not right now. I need to prepare myself." Bud nodded. "Take me by the church, that is if you have time."

"Got all the time we need."

It had been twenty years since I left. A lot had changed. Cannons Campground was hardly distinguishable from Spartanburg. *I bet Blaine's the same way.* However, there were still several landmarks I recognized. Before I knew it we were at Peach Grove Baptist Church.

"Wow! The church sure has grown." There was a new Family Life Center (the ecumenical term for gym), and a new Sunday school building. The sanctuary was at least three times as big. "Can we get in?" Bud gave me one of those "you gotta be kidding" looks and got out of the car.

The sanctuary was simply gorgeous. Candles and greenery adorned all of the window seals. Red and white poinsettias were every where. A huge wreath, covered with white doves, hung just below the baptistery.

"I see the baptistery hasn't changed?"

"Nope. Just as you left it. I can still see you and Joey Gordon splashing around up there, and then you standing there after flooding the whole front of the church and saying "amen." We both burst out laughing.

After a few minutes we went back to Bud's car. "Just think, Bert, we wouldn't have any of this if you'd been any good at preaching." We laughed out loud again.

***

I had basically ignored Christmas for years. I'd send gifts to my family and a card to all of the Anderson's and a few friends but that was about it. But now, back in Cannons Campground, I felt differently. It was like I had come home again, not just to this place but to a state of mind, a place in my heart and my soul that had not be wrecked by cocaine or arrogance or conceit. It was a feeling of warmth, acceptance, and unconditional and unfathomable love.

My purpose for coming was simple: Bud and Charlie asked me to. I was to hold a blessing (Baptist don't christen or baptize babies) for Charlie's first grandchild, a month-old baby girl. I had not come to bury one who had been a constant source of support. I now knew it was also the reason I was here.

"You ready to go?" Bud asked having come to my motel to take me to see Charlie.

"I don't know if I am or not."

"Trust me, it'll be fine."

We didn't talk much on the way. When we got to Bud's house Charlie was sitting up in the hospital bed Bud had gotten from the local hospice group. This was not the Charlie I knew; he was quite simply a ghost of what he was. I tried to be up-beat.

"Mr. Anderson, how you doing?" *How stupid is that-asking a man who could die any minute how he's doing.*

He motioned for me to come closer. Bud explained it took all of his energy to speak. I bent down close to his face.

"Son," *yep, despite his frail frame this was Charlie*, "for a man about to die I'm okay. Will you please call me Charlie?" he said is a whisper.

"Yes sir, Mr. Anderson." We both smiled.

He motioned for Bud who knew exactly what to do. Bud pulled out the drawer of the table next to Charlie's bed and took out an envelope. *Not an envelope. Envelopes from them have money in them. They need to be taking care of Charlie and his family, not me* I thought. But there was no money this time. Inside was a hand written note to me. All it said was "Do this for me." The note was clipped to his instructions on what he wanted at his funeral. I was to do the eulogy. At the end of the instructions was another note to me. "Don't preach-you're no good at it." I couldn't help but snicker out loud

160

which pleased him greatly.

He took my hand and pulled me closer again. "Son, trust me. You'll do fine."

"Thank you, Charlie," I said and kissed him on the forehead.

On the way back to my motel Bud told me about when Charlie was first diagnosed. "He didn't flinch. I was the one who went nuts. You know Charlie. He simply asked 'how long?' When the doc told him a couple of months he stood, stuck out his hand and said 'thanks doc for all you've done' and then left. He didn't say anything until we got in the elevator. By this time I'm about to fall apart. All he said was 'Get Bert, he has to do this. He has to bury me.' Then, just like nothing was wrong, we went about our business. Later that day his first grandchild, Sarah Gayle, was born and from then on his focus was on her.

***

The central part of the Christmas Eve service was the blessing of Sarah Gayle. I had made some notes but things were different now. Just like my thoughts on the plane, I found myself realizing how many things had come full circle. Then I knew what to say and what to do, and made no further preparation.

The sanctuary was packed. It was filled with the glow and warmth of candles, the smell of fresh greenery, and especially with the anticipation of a special baby. All of the Anderson's were in the front pews with Charlie sitting up in his bed right at the center isle next to Bud and Judy.

When the organist finished playing *Jesu, Joy of Man's Desiring,* the minister went to the pulpit and began reading from the second chapter of Luke. He then led everyone in prayer. After the choir finished singing *Glory to God* from Handel's *Messiah* I took the pulpit. At that instant, all the events of the past twenty years rushed around me filling me with a new purpose, a new perspective, a new life.

After reading some passages of scripture and some comments on our purpose that night, I asked Sarah Gayle's parents to join me in front of the Communion Table. I blessed her father, making comparisons to Joseph and Abraham. I blessed her mother making comparisons to Mary, Sarah, and Hagar. Then I asked for Sarah Gayle. After letting her take a few seconds to get used to me holding her I turned to face the congregation.

"Sarah Gayle, you are a savior. You have come to save us: to save us from the cynicism we create about life; to save us from the despair in our hearts and in our souls; to save us from destroying all that we hold dear; and to save us from ourselves.

"Sarah Gayle, you are a teacher. You have come to teach us again that life is big and bright and beautiful; to teach us again the humility and acceptance of a child; to teach us again about true faith and trust.

"Sarah Gayle, you are a messiah. Your linage is

not just the House of Anderson but the House of David and the House of Abraham. The blood of three great religions flows through you the same as it flowed through another baby two thousand years ago. You and all others like you are our hope. You are all that we were, all that we are, and all that we hope to become. You are the filling full of life, now and always."

With Sarah Gayle in my arms I walked over to Charlie. I bent down and helped him cradle her, then I put my hand on Charlie's shoulder.

"Sarah Gayle, you and you Grandfather Charlie are life fulfilled-the beginning and end, the end and beginning; you are one and the same, the Alpha and the Omega. Together you have now come full circle and will do so over and over and over. You are the filling full and fulfillment of life."

I motioned for Sarah Gayle's parents to come to Charlie's bed side.

I faced the congregation again and said, "For unto us a child is born; unto us a son is given. And He shall be called Wonderful, Counselor, the Mighty God, the Everlasting Father, the Prince of Peace. Go in peace and God be with you. Amen."

There was complete silence. No one seemed to know what to do. Then Bud stood and began clapping furiously, and then the whole congregation erupted in a joyous and spontaneous celebration for the lives of Charlie and Sarah Gayle.

***

On the way back to my motel Bud asked "When'd you learn to preach" he said with a great big grin.

"Tonight."

"You pick that up at that fancy New York seminary?"

"No sir. You and Charlie taught me.

As we drove Bud told me their minister was retiring in June and wondered if I could check around for someone good to take his place. I said I still had some friends in minister circles who still claimed me and that I'd be glad to check with them.

"Bud, may I come for breakfast with your family tomorrow? And may I borrow Charlie's car for a few days?"

"Of course to both" he said.

After Christmas breakfast the next morning I asked Bud to walk me out to Charlie's car. Bud handed me the car keys and asked "Where you going, not that it's any of my business?"

"I seem to remember there's place in Blaine, Tennessee that serves a great Christmas dinner. I'll be back in a few days. If Charlie dies before then just call me and I'll be right here."

As I opened the door to get in I said "And by the way, I'll take the job."

Bud didn't expect that at all.

"Don't worry, Bud. Trust me. It'll be fine."

ALSO BY STEVEN ROBERTS

CHRISTMAS ON DEERY STREET & OTHER SEASONAL STORIES

Whether it's the plight of a young soldier snow-bound in a train station on Christmas Eve who's befriended by a big-bellied, gold-toothed janitor; or a ten year old girl with bare feet and a booming voice who steals the Christmas pageant; or a precocious young boy who cuts his initials in the cat's fur and completely wraps himself in strands of Christmas light; or the first act of rebellion by the oldest of seven children against her mother, whose strong will is only surpassed by her big heart, you will be captured and enthralled by these delightful and charming Christmas tales. While each of these are separate stories they all weave together to echo the messages and miracles of Christmas. Christmas on Deery Street reminds us of what's best in all of us, not just at Christmas but always. "Steven Roberts is a master of the gentle O'Henry twist ending and creating tableaux that are as real and moving as any Norman Rockwell painting...Christmas on Deery Street is a wonderful celebration of holidays, family, and life" Ellen Tanner Marsh, New York Times bestselling author.

Learn more at:
www.outskirtspress.com/ChristmasonDeeryStreet

Printed in the United States
90677LV00001B/172-999/A